TO LIVE WITH FEAR

Whilst working in remote South America, Robin Stanton hears that his beloved sister, Carol, has committed suicide. He refuses to believe this and returns to England. He starts to probe into Carol's death, becoming more and more convinced that she was murdered. He finds her diaries, which lead him to think that she was being set up by British Intelligence — or someone more sinister. Meanwhile, he falls in love with Jackie Fremington — but is she more involved than she admits?

Books by Judy Chard
in the Linford Romance Library:

PERSON UNKNOWN
TO BE SO LOVED
ENCHANTMENT
APPOINTMENT WITH DANGER
BETRAYED
THE SURVIVORS

JUDY CHARD

TO LIVE WITH FEAR

Complete and Unabridged

LINFORD
Leicester

First published in Great Britain in 1985

First Linford Edition
published 2002

British Library CIP Data

Chard, Judy
    To live with fear.—Large print ed.—
Linford romance library
1. Love stories
2. Large type books
I. Title
823.9'14 [F]

ISBN 0–7089–9815

Published by
F. A. Thorpe (Publishing)
Anstey, Leicestershire

Set by Words & Graphics Ltd.
Anstey, Leicestershire
Printed and bound in Great Britain by
T. J. International Ltd., Padstow, Cornwall

This book is printed on acid-free paper

1

The man stood looking down the steep hillside to the green valley far below. He could just make out a mule winding its way up the track.

The grass ran like sunlight up to the grey crags around him, the early morning sun made the air shimmer over the coloured fields below.

For a moment he wished Carol were with him, his beloved little sister. She would have loved the grandeur, the starkness. His hand felt the thin tissue of the air letter in his pocket, a letter that bubbled over with life and love for it; with chatter about London and how she had grown to like it.

'Remember — you've got a key to the flat. Come any time. It's so long since I saw you. We'll have a party, a real rave-up.' He could almost hear her say the words, his lips curved into a smile as he thought of her, pictured her.

Now his eyes returned their glance to the mule. It must be coming his way, it was only a few hundred yards away.

Suddenly, for no reason, he felt apprehension, a kind of distant aura it had brought with it. The peasant on its back could be distinguished in a brightly coloured poncho, the inevitable straw hat.

A heron flew white against the intense blue of the sky, and away in the distance, wheeling and sliding down the thermals, the condors . . .

Sometimes he wondered why he had chosen this country to work in, to live in . . . nothing could have been further from the life he had led in the Navy — a life he had enjoyed, that he thought would go on until he retired. Then one day his ship had put into port in Valdavero in South America. There he had caught an obscure, tropical bug and been whisked off to hospital. His ship had had to sail without him.

He was ill for months; in fact at one

time he had lost the will to live; and then he had thought of Carol, and what a love she had for life, a joy in living; he remembered her philosophy that everyone should be grateful at least for being given the chance to be alive in such a wonderful world.

At last he had recovered, but the virulence of the illness had left him with a weak heart and he had been invalided out of the Navy. While all this had been happening, he had spent time in wandering round the altiplano — the remote mountain area of the country, and it had appealed to something in his make up so that he had lost his heart — and sometimes he thought his head too, to its extraordinary type of stark beauty, its primitive people, and their way of life, and had found himself a job with a mining company who were exploring for new sites. He had been an engineering officer in the Navy so really there was no problem, the nomadic life suited him and the time he had for books and music. The people too appealed to him with their innocence and freshness, as yet unspoiled by civilisation. Now he had come to this remote plain, accessible only by mule or llama train, carrying the bare necessities of bivouac tent and tinned food.

Unfortunately his radio had been destroyed when one of the mules had slipped and fallen, losing its load into a deep ravine. But he wasn't very concerned, there was no reason anyone would want to communicate with him, and at the end of next week he would be back in Valdavero with the results and analysis the company wanted.

The mule had reached him now. The peasant held out an envelope.

'Buenos días. For the señor — Señor Robin Stanton. A message from England,' he said with great importance as though it had come from outer space.

For a moment Robin hesitated. The apprehension he had experienced early returned with increased force. At last he held out his hand, 'I am Señor Stanton.'

He took the envelope, turning it over

4

in his hand, somehow reluctant to open it. Why should anyone in England send him a telegram — and for what reason? The telephone wires were often down between the base and the nearest village, this man was probably a messenger they kept in reserve, often mule power was still more reliable than modern technology. Often the wires were cut by roving parties of bandits.

The man leant forwards, 'It is bad news, Señor?' His tone was hopeful. Robin had forgotten his presence. He felt in his pocket and put a coin in the dirty palm. The man put it immediately into his mouth, clenching his coca-stained teeth on it, grinning.

Slowly, unwillingly, Robin slit open the envelope. His premonition of disaster so strong it was almost tangible.

For a moment the words danced in front of his eyes. He passed his hand over them, then read the words again, pretending to himself they might have changed.

But they hadn't, they were still there in stark reality —

DEEPLY REGRET INFORM YOU CAROL DEAD. PLEASE COME, LOVE NORA.

The unwritten words in the plea were so full of emotion, they touched his heart so that the tears sprang to his eyes.

It was a mistake of course, a terrible, ghastly mistake someone had made. Not Nora, she was too meticulous over the smallest detail to have made a blunder like that. No, somewhere between England and this remote rocky place, the words had become twisted. Why, he had a letter from Carol in his pocket saying that life was good and vivid, alive.

The peasant had turned away, lost interest, anxious only to return to the village where he could convert the coin into coca to bring blessed oblivion from poverty and hunger, the ever-present threat of bandits.

Robin went into his tent. He had to think. His assistant, Peter Coombes, had gone up further into the interior where another new shaft was being opened. Apart from a couple of servants, he was completely alone on the site. But there was no question of what he had to do, where his priorities lay.

He scribbled a note to Peter and gave it to one of the men to take to him. He explained the position as best he could, saying he had no idea when he would be back, but when he got to the airport he would arrange with head office for his replacement as soon as possible.

It was difficult to concentrate, to think of what had to be done. Yet, in a way, he welcomed the necessity, for it distracted his mind a little from the enormity of the words, printed coldly on the paper of the telegram . . . Carol dead . . . it just couldn't be.

He packed his few belongings and slung the case on the back of a mule.

The light seemed metallically intense now; he could see, far below, some llamas on a narrow ledge. It was odd how he observed every detail as though he would never come back, and wanted to imprint it on memory. Walter de la Mare's words came into his mind — 'Look thy last on all things lovely, every hour'. How often Carol had quoted those words when they had seen some specially beautiful scene or painting. The thought brought a lump to his throat. He had to brush away the mist of tears that filled his eyes. He just couldn't imagine the world — a world — without his sister. They had been like the two halves of a whole in many ways; the natural bond strengthened because their parents had been killed in a pile-up on the motorway one foggy November night. Carol had been seven and he, ten. Gravely he had told her then, when the terrible truth eventually sunk in, that he would always look after her.

It was strange really, because often

she had turned out to be the strong one in the relationship. They had been moved from one foster home to another, often because they would not be parted and foster parents only wanted one child, not two. There had been a time when he had even wished they were both dead, and said so, and Carol had flown into one of her rare tempers, telling him life was all that mattered, quoting Borrow — 'There's night and day brother, both sweet things; sun, moon and stars brother, all sweet things, there's likewise a wind on the hearth. Life is very sweet brother, who would wish to die?'

He had felt bitterly ashamed, also reassured. They had shared a love of poetry of music and reading. And then Nora had come into their lives.

She lived in Wolverhampton, at least just outside in a small village. She ran a kind of farm, although it was certain she never made any money, for when the cows became barren, they were pensioned off until they died of old age, eating their heads off. The chicken and ducks all had names, as had the geese, none of which were ever killed.

'They're part of the family, you don't eat your friends, unless you are a cannibal!' Nora would say as Lulu, the 20-year-old bantam, flew on to her shoulders making her look like some kind of latter-day Captain Flint.

Above all she loved kids, everything that lived and breathed was a gift from God, life itself a sacred trust; all this had brushed off on Carol and Robin and when taken under her wing, they blossomed into the kind of people that only Nora could produce. She was mother and father to them, and to all the children she took into her home.

'Talk about the old woman who lived in a shoe!' people used to say. But everyone in the village loved her, and would have given her any help she needed, but it was something she never sought. 'Neither a lender nor a borrower be,' she used to say, with tongue in cheek, as yet another neighbour came for a 'a few eggs till Monday, Nora love . . . ' or 'could I just have a pinta till the milkman comes?' and always she refused to be paid back because of her principles, as she called them.

Now Robin's mind buzzed like a hive of angry bees with memories, thoughts, bewilderment — such bewilderment as the plane approached Heathrow. It was partly the memory of the letter and Carol's happiness, her lively chatter. Written, as he compared the dates, on the day Nora had sent the telegram, and which had been delayed for several weeks because of the remoteness of his camp. It must have been an accident of some kind, that was the only explanation he could think of. But why hadn't Nora said so in the telegram? Why did it just say 'Carol dead.' Even repeating the words brought the tears to his eyes again.

The plane circled the huge airport. Other silver machines stood on the runways, people ran hither and thither like frantic ants, shining streams of cars strung out in all directions. He'd been abroad so long, in the peace and tranquillity of the altiplano, he felt confused.

It didn't take him long to get through Customs with only hand baggage. Immediately he made his way to a phonebox. Even to hear Nora's voice would he balm, and to hear her tell him it was all wrong, a mistake.

He still tried to tell himself it must be so.

2

It was a long time before the phone was answered. He began to think he must have the wrong number. But at last he heard the receiver lifted. With relief he said, 'Aunt Nora, it's Robin . . . ' but a voice at the other end cut him short.

'Mrs Lunt isn't here.'

It was like a slap in the face on top of everything else. He had been nearly at the end of his tether, the thought of hearing Nora's warm voice had been like a sheet anchor.

'Not there?' he knew his tone was sharp. There was a pause, he could hear the person at the other end breathing.

'What do you mean?'

'She's gone to London. Don't know when she'll be back.'

'But she never goes to London.' Directly he'd said the words he realised how futile they sounded. 'I mean . . . '

13

'She had to go. The police came, it's an inquest . . . '

'An inquest? I don't understand. What are you talking about? Who are you?'

His tone was brusque. The answer came slowly, slightly cagey even.

'I'm looking after things for Mrs Lunt. That's all I know.' He was desperate.

'Please don't ring off. The person the inquest is about . . . ' he hesitated, finding it difficult to bring himself to say the words . . . 'I mean, the deceased — I think she may be my sister. Please help me. Can you tell me how to find Aunt Nora?'

'Oh it's you, she did say you might be in touch. You'll have to hang on while I find the address.'

The minutes ticked away. He had to find more change for the phone. He could feel the sweat running under his armpits. The July sun was scalding, heat shimmered from the tarmac.

'You there?' the voice returned . . . he

wrote down the address of a hotel in Kensington.

London radiated heat under the July sun. The streets were dusty, old newspapers and litter lay in the gutters, girls in summer frocks strolled in the parks the taxi passed. Girls who reminded him of Carol . . .

At the hotel reception desk the girl gave him a curious look when he asked for Mrs Lunt. She went to the rack which held residents' letters and, with maddening slowness, searched the cubbyholes.

'What name did you say?'

'Stanton, Robin Stanton. I thought she might have left me a note, expected me to come to find her.' He was on the edge of desperation once more. At last she handed it to him. With trembling fingers he tore it open. It was very brief.

'Dear Robin, Not having had a reply to my telegram, I can only think you have not received it. In case you do turn up by some miracle, I have left a note of where I've gone. Today they are holding an inquest on darling Carol. If you get this before I'm back, get a taxi and give him the address of the court, otherwise you'll never find it. I still can't believe it. Yours Nora.'

He stood holding it for a moment as he had the telegram three days ago. He still couldn't understand it. Still she hadn't told him how Carol had died. Her writing was big and round, like a child's. They'd always laughed because she had made an effort once to keep accounts, but there had been so few words and figures on each page, she had given up in despair. Round, generous — like Nora herself.

He felt the girl watching him.

'Could you get me a taxi please?'

She stared at him, 'You can't order them just like that, you have to go into the street and find one.'

'Oh I see, thanks.' He'd never felt so desolate, so alone in all his life. Even the altiplano seemed more friendly than this alien city with its people who couldn't care less.

16

To add to this feeling, the building, when he reached it, was impersonal, cold, even in the summer heat. An official directed him to the coroner's court. He hardly noticed his surroundings as he went in. The courtroom seemed full, sunlight streamed in through the dusty windows, motes danced in the golden beams. He felt lightheaded as if it were all a dream, or he had a fever and would soon wake. He found a seat near the door and glanced round. Somewhere Nora must be sitting, but he couldn't see her.

The coroner had heard all the evidence. He felt more confused than ever. He knew little about the law; was there always an inquest if someone young and healthy died? Surely not. Then Carol's death had to have been an accident — a car accident. That must be it.

The coroner was obviously summing up from all the evidence that had been gathered over the past few weeks ... few weeks? Police evidence was read out. A dark girl had been coming out of the witness box as he came into the court. Somehow he got the impression that whatever she had said hadn't been very popular with the coroner, or some of the other people in the body of the court. One man was frowning and tapping his teeth with a gold pen.

'So, Carol Stanton, the deceased, was found on the evening of the 15th June in the garage below her flat in Cherry Tree Mews, Chelsea, in this jurisdiction. Medical evidence has been brought to prove that she died of carbon monoxide poisoning,' he hesitated a moment and consulted his notes, 'although at the time of the discovery, the car engine had run itself to a standstill?' He looked over his rimless glasses at a policeman who stood up and said, 'That is correct, your Honour.'

'We have also had evidence from Miss Stanton's colleagues who worked with her,' he paused again and this time

18

cleared his throat, 'it seems the young lady was having some kind of clandestine affair with a man already married, who has been referred to in the evidence as Mr X. I am informed that as the young woman was not pregnant at the time, that no useful purpose can be served by disclosing his name as he had no direct connection with Miss Stanton's death.'

No one made any comment. A rustle like a long drawn out sigh went round the court. Then someone coughed. For a moment Robin felt the whole court waited with baited breath for someone to say something. He himself was so stunned by the words he had heard, he was not only speechless, but he felt as if his whole body had become paralysed, and yet he wanted to stand up and shout at these people, tell them the kind of person Carol had been, nothing like the impression this man was giving by the tone of his voice, by what he felt were half-hidden innuendoes . . .

'The verdict of the court, based on

the evidence given, is of suicide while the balance of the mind was disturbed.'

Robin really had no idea what happened next. He sat where he was while people surged around him; talking, brushing past him, leaving the courtroom. At last he struggled to his feet. He only had one thought in mind now, he must find Aunt Nora, talk to her, tell her what they both already knew, that it was completely, utterly impossible that Carol could have taken her own life . . . 'Life is very sweet, brother. Who would wish to die?' He could almost hear her repeating those words.

Nora stood in the passage, white, looking ten years older, her hat askew. He had never seen her in a hat before, suddenly it made him want to laugh. Or cry. Strange how akin the two emotions were.

She turned and saw him. For a moment, as if the sun had come from behind a cloud, her face lit up. With a little cry she went into his arms. He held her close, the warmth of her body through the thin summer dress, a comfort. The sweet, clean country smell so familiar, bringing so many memories of summer days in hayfields, of hands stained scarlet from picking strawberries . . .

'I need a cuppa love. We'll go back to the hotel. Thank God you've come. I thought you never would.'

He knew this was no time for explanations, for apologies.

The lounge was empty. Nora sank down into a chair; her plump figure, resisting all restraint by her old-fashioned corset, seemed to be spilling out in every direction. Her hair had escaped from her attempt to pin it up, and her face shone with sweat and misery.

Robin found a girl who brought them a tray of tea, looking at them without any particular interest or curiosity, but at least the tea was hot and strong.

Nora dumped her hat. She looked at him like a dog that has been whipped;

entreaty, disbelief in her eyes.

She kicked off her shoes, and for some reason this brought a small measure of comfort to Robin. It was such a homely gesture; Nora would be able to make it all right, to tell him it wasn't true, that the whole thing was a nightmare and in a moment his sister would burst into the room, as she always had done, like a small tornado, unable ever to do anything slowly or with dignity. Laughing always at pomposity.

She must.

He longed to say, 'Tell me it isn't true.' But he knew in his heart it was — true that Carol was dead — not true she had taken her own life; that, never.

Nora started to speak, her voice low as if they were in the presence of the dead even in this sleazy hotel lounge with its smell of dust and cabbage water. She told him how the police had come, how she too couldn't believe it.

'They wanted me to identify her you see, love. Being the nearest of kin, not next exactly, only you are that. But you were so far away. I began to think you'd never come.' Tears in her voice . . . He put his arm round her, longing to drop his head on her shoulders, but feeling she already had enough to stand on their breadth without his adding to the burden.

'I know, I'm so sorry. I was up in the hills, the altiplano. I know it seems ridiculous in the age of the jet, of electronics, instant communication, but that's how it was. I came as soon as I got your telegram . . . '

He was about to tell her of Carol's letter, the bubbling, lovely letter he'd received, but he knew it would upset her even more. Neither could he tell her of the time when he had wanted to opt out, and Carol had laughed him out of it, that it could even be considered as such a possibility — never . . .

'We took her home to bury her — when they'd let us.' He'd never heard bitterness in Nora's voice before; she went on, 'Once the coroner chap was satisfied with the evidence. We had to wait for that . . . it didn't seem right, leaving her in that dreadful place. I knew she'd want to rest in our churchyard, in the village. I hope you don't mind, love?'

He squeezed her hand. 'Of course not. You had to do what you thought best. I'm only sorry I wasn't here to help, I'll never forgive myself.' Now he dropped his head on his hands and now it was her turn to comfort, to reassure.

'Don't worry about it. So soon as you can get away, come home, and see where we laid her. At least now I'll be able to leave the job of clearing up her little flat to you.' She pushed herself wearily to her feet, 'I'll have to go and rest up a little now, love. I have to catch an early train, can't leave Tracey too long. She's a good kid, but you know what these girls are, a bit scatty.' She gave a weak grin, knowing how they had always teased her about using that word. She had so many words he would always connect with her — sleazy, tatty, seedy, all part of the family life they had with her.

He watched her climb the stairs, all the spring gone from her step, and went to the reception desk. Yes, they had a room. Was it a double he wanted? The girl looked at him curiously, trying to assess the relationship between this very dishy young man, and the queer old girl who'd been with them a couple of days, attending some inquest or other. A girl had committed suicide. She wasn't particularly interested, it happened all the time. It only became interesting when it was someone you knew. Probably something to do with the recession and unemployment. Everyone blamed everything on those two factors now.

Robin went out into the airless street. He hailed a taxi and gave the driver the address of Carol's flat.

The mews was gaily painted, each flat and garage in different colours. There were tubs and pots of bright flowers, window boxes as if each occupant vied with the other for the most colourful display. He got out the key and put it in the lock, suddenly realising that it must have been behind the yellow garage door they had found her . . . he wondered if the car was still there and if he would have to dispose of it . . . A voice behind him said.

'Good God! Can't you people ever leave things alone. Aren't you ever done with your nosy enquiries, your questions, probing . . . '

He swung round. A girl stood on the cobbled stones, she was small and dark, her hair a curtain about her shoulders; her eyes deep blue like zircons, but now they flashed like steel, and even though she looked tired and hot, there was no doubt she was beautiful.

'I don't know to what people you are referring, but as it happens I'm Robin Stanton . . . ' he paused and then stumbled over the words, 'Carol was my sister.'

The girl looked as if she had been slapped in the face. For a moment he thought she was going to burst into tears, then she said softly. 'I'm so sorry, so dreadfully sorry.' She stretched out her hand in a helpless gesture, and then dropped it again, and added without looking at him, 'What a terrible way to speak. I'm Jackie Fremington. I live opposite where . . . ' her voice died away.

'I saw you in the court didn't I?'

She nodded, then said slowly, 'Before you go in there, come and have a cup of coffee. I feel I owe you that at least for my awful greeting.'

If he were honest, he would admit he had dreaded going into the flat, and any excuse for a delay was welcome.

'Well thanks, if you're sure.'

Jackie made coffee and he sat on the comfortable, chintz-covered sofa. There wasn't much furniture, but it was well chosen. The walls were painted white, some rugs hung from a rail. There was a cane chair and table with a glass top. In one corner, a hi-fi set.

'Have you been in Carol's flat before?

She told me you worked somewhere in the wilds of South America?' She smiled at him tentatively over the rim of her cup. She reminded him somehow of a small animal, ready all the time to scuttle away and hide.

'I've been abroad a long time, she wasn't in this flat last time I was home, so I have never been inside. She moved in soon after I left.'

'Of course she had a much better job than me. Very posh, somewhere in Whitehall I think. I'm only a school teacher, primary.'

'Yes, she told me she had some kind of courier work I think.'

'I didn't really know her very well, I thought it was something to do with the Department of the Environment. Civil Service anyway.' She paused a moment then said 'More coffee?'

Reluctantly he got to his feet. 'No, thanks all the same. I have to get this job done, go over and . . . ' he paused. He wasn't quite sure what he had to do. Go through Carol's things he supposed.

He would have to decide what to do with them — clothes, make-up. Take them up to Nora's. It was a furnished flat so there would only be personal things to deal with he supposed.

'Thanks. That saved my life,' he grinned at her. She smiled back, hesitantly, tentatively. 'Sorry we didn't meet under happier conditions.'

'Yes.' She opened the door, 'Perhaps later, when things are a bit straightened out.'

The flat was so typical of Carol it hurt afresh. Even her perfume seemed to hang faintly on the air. Although the basic furniture was good quality, and in fine condition, she had impressed her own personality upon it with little touches — pieces of beautiful pottery, pictures in soft pastels — always her favourite medium.

He picked up a photograph someone had taken of them both with Nora. Puppies and kittens littered the ground, a goose with outstretched neck stood honking in one corner.

A pile of records lay on a chair where she must have left them, almost as if she had been interrupted. One was even out of its sleeve and on the turntable. Vivaldi . . .

The white painted shelves held books. Hundreds of books lined the walls. She must have bought extra shelves to hold them all.

Some had faded covers and spines, obviously much loved and often read. He took down a collection of Robert Frost's poems. They had been to the Round House to hear someone read from it once, with a background of music. They had fallen under the spell of his beauty of writing, his phrases, his words, and one snowy night in the country, Carol had stopped as she climbed a stile and recited his words 'The woods are lovely, dark and deep. But I have promises to keep, and miles to go before I sleep.'

The more he thought about and remembered her, the more he felt her presence in the little flat for some reason he became uneasily aware that something was wrong. Never could Carol have had an affair with someone else's husband. If she had taken her own life, then something, or someone, had driven her to it.

There was a book on the coffee table which he remembered well. He bent to pick it up and his foot caught against something. A pair of shoes lying by the chair, just as she had left them, one on its side, as though they had been kicked off, and waited for their owner to return.

The book fell from his grasp. As it did so, a piece of paper fluttered to the floor. The book lay open. On the fly leaf he saw that he had written the words 'To Little Sis. Be Happy. Rob.' and the date.

He looked at the piece of paper. George Borrow's words, which she had once quoted to him, were written in her handwriting. 'There's night and day, brother, both sweet things; Life is very sweet, brother. Who would wish to die?'

His eye travelled down the page. Underneath were columns of numbers and letters. At first they didn't mean much and he was about to shut the book and put it back. Suddenly something about the columns rang a bell. As kids they had a secret code. He ran a pencil along the numbers and letters. L1 W2 Le 2. He counted the words, the line, the letters. They made the letter 'I'. He went on, L1 W8 Le 3 and 4 . . . so it went.

At last he had the complete sentence. Four words.

'I Live with Fear.'

3

As Rob read the words he had deciphered with the old code from their childhood days, 'I live with fear', he felt once again that his sister must have had some kind of emotional problem, something had been preying on her mind. Something very odd had been going on, of that he was sure. Had she perhaps been let down by this unnamed lover? That in itself seemed strange. He was torn between anger, frustration and pity, but whatever it was he was determined now that he would find out what had gone wrong with her life.

He glanced round the room again as if it held the secret, the key to the situation. He hadn't yet started tidying up her things, and he wondered if he could ask Jackie to help, but she hadn't been really close to Carol, it seemed a cheek to ask. Anyway, now he had to see that Nora got off home. There was nothing she could do in London and she would be happier back on her own stamping ground he knew.

For the moment he had decided he would say nothing to her of his vague, unformulated thoughts, for that is all they were. He had to stand back from the situation, look at it in perhaps a more detached way. He was too close, too shocked, his judgment impaired. His mouth was set in a grim line as he went out into the warm, evening sunshine. The mews dreamed in a kind of golden peace. It was quite impossible to believe violence, perhaps horror and hate could even exist in such a place.

Once more his eyes were drawn to the primrose-coloured garage doors; one of the 'up-and-over' kind. He had to see . . . he pressed the handle. To his surprise it wasn't locked and swung open. For a moment his heart missed a beat at what he might be about to see . . .

There was nothing. It was completely

empty. Swept and garnished, as Nora would have said. No dust on the floor, no pools of oil, as if it had never been used. He wondered where the car was. Who would have removed it? The police he supposed. Had they the right to keep it? How ignorant he was of the procedure under the present circumstances. Should he consult a solicitor? But what would he say — there was nothing, nothing tangible, only surmise.

The evening sun crept through the open door. Now he noticed some marks on the floor, in the tiny skim of dust that was left, highlighted by the suns rays. They seemed vaguely familiar, the marks. Then he realised they were the kind of ridges left by a domestic vacuum cleaner. Why on earth should the police vacuum the floor of a garage where someone had committed suicide? What could they be looking for? Was it the forensic people who had taken dust away to examine? It couldn't be. The coroner had said it was a straightforward case of suicide, or words to that effect. Rob was beginning to think there was less and less straight-forward about the whole affair.

He nibbled the corner of his thumb as ideas started to form vaguely on the edge of his mind.

He got a taxi back to the hotel. Nora had packed her case. She sat now in the small lounge, her hands folded, some kind of peace at least seemed to have returned, but he knew how she fretted against inactivity. She looked up and smiled as he came into the room.

'I wondered where you'd taken yourself off to. I had a good sleep, never thought I should. My train goes in an hour. Will you come to the station with me, love?'

'Of course.' He bent and kissed her cheek, soft as a child's. He knew the tears were not far away. She pressed his arm with her fingers.

'Give us a hand then. My back's playing up something shocking.' She smoothed down the skirt of the wool dress. It seemed strange to see her thus.

Always she wore slacks, sweaters, what she called comfortable clothes. She was a comfortable kind of person, and even the modest finery she had put on for her stay in London was as foreign to her as would have been a wig and false eyelashes.

They didn't talk much on the way to the station. She was watching the unfamiliar streets, the people hurrying along like demented ants. He knew she felt the driver could hear what they said, and she wasn't going to talk 'family business' in front of him.

At the station he changed her second class return for a first, and found her an empty compartment, bought some magazines and a box of her favourite chocolates.

'You do spoil me,' she sighed, 'wish you didn't work so far away, love. Come home before you leave for South America again. Stay a little while, will you?'

He bent and kissed her, then sat beside her. There were a few minutes before the train left. The compartment was still empty.

'Of course. I don't quite know how long I'll be in London,' he hesitated. It was the truth. He wasn't sure what he meant to do, what he could do, all he knew was he had no intention of telling her at the moment of his suspicions. They were far too vague, too nebulous. Each time he tried to think them out, to pin them down, they vanished like wraiths of mist. He knew all she would say would be, 'what is done is done. Maybe we shouldn't interfere with the Lord's plans for us.' She had always been one for minding her own business, except where injustice and cruelty occurred. He knew she was thinking that Carol was dead and nothing would bring her back. She had lost one beloved child, now she feared somehow for the child that was alive — her Rob.

The facts were right he knew, hard to accept but somehow, like a dog with a rat, he had to worry this thing out to the end, however nebulous it might be, whatever it might cost, however long it might take. There was something he had to do; he wasn't even sure yet what it was . . .

She looked at him now, and as always with that candid gaze on him, he found it difficult to hide his feelings. 'Is it some kind of work connected with your job that will keep you here after you've cleared up the flat?' He glanced away, the silence heavy between them. Somehow all the cacophony of sound, of trains, of shouting people and the rumbling of the luggage trolleys, passed over them. It was as if they were alone in a small world of their own.

Now he looked at her, patting her hand, 'Not exactly, but it's nothing for you to worry about, and I'd rather not talk about it just at this moment.'

She gave him a shrewd look, one of the kind that he and Carol had called 'old-fashioned', and he knew she knew just as if he had put it into words that his mind was uneasy, but all she said was,

'Take care, love, please. I couldn't bear any more, not just now. Mind what you're about.'

He grinned, 'You know what they say, the devil looks after his own.'

Now it was her turn to smile, 'You always said that when you got into scrapes as a tacker, and I told you it was the Lord, not the devil.'

He lit a cigarette, something he seldom did now. He looked at her through the fragrant blue smoke. 'Did Carol manage to get home often?'

She nodded, 'She was so good about that. Every second weekend without fail,' she hesitated, 'that is until a few months ago. After that, well, it seems with some kind of new job she had, she was so busy, even working weekends. There were phonecalls, but somehow it wasn't like her, there would be excuses all the time about why she couldn't get up here any more. I didn't like to press her, everyone has to live their own lives o'course. Like you going abroad,' she added with a subtle dig at him. He covered her hand with his, feeling the rough skin, the callouses, which somehow filled him with a great tenderness.

'I know. I'm sorry, but there's something about South America, and I love my job. It wouldn't be difficult to find one like it anywhere else, in that kind of terrain.'

'I know too,' she grinned at him, 'it's only an old woman having her little joke.'

The guard was banging the doors along the train now. Only a few seconds left, but he had to know . . .

'Did Carol have a boyfriend back home in Blisford?'

Nora nodded. 'She did as a matter of fact,' she paused a moment, 'that's why I think all that was nonsense they talked about someone in London, a married man; it just wasn't her nature.'

'Tell me about this chap.'

'Frank Barton. A nice young man, quite ordinary, like the rest of us, but he's worked hard, managed to get together a nice little business, a small garage. Does repairs and that kind of thing. Folk need their cars looked after now they've taken off all the buses, and Frank's reliable; if he says he's done a job to your car, then he's done it.'

The whistle blew. Rob got to his feet, catching her hand in his, hugging her to him.

'When are you coming up?' He knew the tears weren't far away, but she wouldn't let them fall while he was there.

'Maybe sooner than you think.' He jumped onto the platform as the train started to move. It gathered speed and rounded the corner. He stood with his hand raised, watching the gallant white flap of her handkerchief until she was out of sight. He hadn't missed the anxiety in her eyes as he left her. For a moment he felt like a child again, bereft by her absence, alone — alone in a hostile, strange city. He shrugged his shoulders. He was being a fool . . . an utter idiot. No one was after his blood, no one was hostile, as a matter of fact probably hardly anyone in the city even knew of his existence. What had he to fear anyway? Perhaps it was just the memory of Carol's words which somehow seemed to have come from the other side of the grave, 'I live with fear' . . .

Now that Nora had gone he couldn't stomach the idea of staying in the hotel. There was no reason why he shouldn't use Carol's flat.

The receptionist was still sulky and unhelpful. Perhaps the city is alien after all, he thought, as he cancelled his room and wrote out a cheque for the two nights he had booked.

He rang the landlord of Carol's flat whose name Nora had given him. The man told him the lease ran for another month. 'It's entirely up to you whether you keep it on or not Mr Stanton.' Rob could tell from his tone of voice that he would be quite relieved. It wasn't to everyone's taste to move into a flat where a suicide had taken place. Murder — well people didn't seem to object to that, they had a kind of macabre fascination, but suicide was something else. However, public memory was short, soon there would be another scandal, another violence and they would have forgotten. In a month's time when the lease was up, someone would be only too glad to take the nice central little mews flat.

Once more he took a taxi and let himself in through the pale yellow door of the flat. There was no light on in Jackie's flat. He supposed she was out. Someone as young and pretty could hardly ever be short of dates.

4

Once again he stood gazing round the lounge. Then he went over to the window and looked into the mews below. Long shadows filled the narrow street, the scent of geraniums in the window boxes and tubs below was wafted to him on the evening air. One or two people hurried along the cobbles, going about their business, leading ordinary normal lives, probably unaware of what had occurred in the flat as they passed. The dark blankness of Jackie's windows opposite made him feel an even more acute loneliness. Impatient with himself, he turned away. He had to make a start somewhere he supposed. He had promised Nora to pack up Carol's clothes and send them back to Blisford, or take them when he visited.

'She would have wanted them to go

to someone who really needs them, and I know just the person,' she had said. Dear Nora, she always knew someone in need, someone she could help. 'You keep her books and china and paintings, love, if you want. One day you'll have a girl of your own, a home here I hope, not out in that heathen place. I'll keep them till you need them. They'd be better at home than in a warehouse . . . nasty damp old places.'

He had agreed. Any help, any suggestions gratefully received. He still felt so confused, so unbelieving. He found it difficult to think clearly, to be rational. He would have to get some cases, tea chests, if such things were still available. He doubted if the ubiquitous tea bag came from overseas in chests, but he supposed he could find something.

He knew no one in London, had lost all touch, all contact from having been away so long. He just didn't know where to start, whom to approach. Could he trespass on Jackie's good nature? She seemed a nice kid, well, more than a kid, she must be about Carol's age, but different as chalk from cheese. Carol had been outgoing, the complete extrovert. Jackie, he sensed, was rather a private person, shy.

He put on the kettle. It was getting late. He'd bought a packet of sandwiches on the station. He found a tin of instant coffee, a carton of long life milk. He opened the fridge. Someone had been through it, taken everything out and switched it off. He felt a little prickle of unease at the idea of strangers in the flat, but of course the police would have been there. Already he had come to look on it as his own. He had a momentary sickness at the idea of 'them', whoever they might be, turning over Carol's things, and yet, apart from the fridge, nothing seemed to have been disturbed or out of place.

The coffee was comforting. He sat at the small table and drew out a notebook. He tore a sheet out and laid it on the glass top. Where to begin . . . ?

He wrote two headings side by side at the top of the page, and drew columns. One was headed NORTH (Blisford, Nora's village,) the other was the one word LONDON. Then, as if making a family tree, under North he drew two subdivisions. One was headed Frank Barton, the other, simply Nora.

He sat and looked at the words for a little while. Funny Carol never mentioned this Frank Barton in any of her letters. Could it mean anything? And yet Nora had said he was a nice lad. He'd never known her wrong. He sighed and his pencil moved to the London side.

Now he made several sub-headings — 'Police,' 'Work', 'Mr X', and 'Jackie'. Slowly he drew a line linking 'Mr X' and Frank Barton in the other column. Was it possible they were one and the same? He added a question mark. But they had hinted the man was married, in public life. He hesitated. Should he eliminate Frank? No, not for the moment. He needed all the facts he could dig out, and heaven knew they were few enough.

He sat staring at the paper until the letters danced in front of his eyes. Those were the routes he would follow. Perhaps in that order. The police — somehow he felt the evidence they had given hadn't been full, detailed enough. Work — he still didn't actually know who Carol had worked for. He wished he'd brought her letters with him from South America, although he knew them pretty well by heart, he couldn't remember her ever having mentioned specifically what she did. Would Jackie know any contacts, or even which office he could go to where he might talk to some of the girls she had worked with — and the men. Mr X — he seemed to be well protected, hidden. There didn't seem much hope of contacting him, unless one of the other two headings helped out, either deliberately or by chance. He tapped his teeth with his pencil.

It seemed the obvious thing to do

first was to contact the police about the car. After all, that was not their property, legally it was his now and he could demand it back. There didn't seem to be much doubt about that. Suddenly he realised he was dead tired. He drank the last of the cold coffee. He hadn't thought about actual bed, where he would sleep. He knew there was only one bedroom in the flat, he'd seen the half-open door, but he hadn't been in. He didn't know if there were any bedclothes. Oh well, he was used to sleeping rough, he could doss down on the sofa if necessary.

He went through into the bedroom, pausing for a moment on the threshold. Everything again was neat, tidy, undisturbed. He forced himself to open the cupboard, the drawers. Her clothes were all there; not many, granted, but she never had been one to spend much on her appearance. The bed was made up, He turned back the counterpane. A shiver ran along his nerves and a lump came into his throat. A pale blue silk nightdress was neatly folded, just as Carol must have left it.

He turned away with an exclamation of impatience. For some reason now he cursed afresh that he had not come home sooner, if only he had known earlier. Precious time had been lost because it had taken so long for him to receive the message. Would someone who intended suicide, whose balance of the mind was disturbed, fold their nightdress neatly, make their bed?

Much to his surprise, he slept soundly, although when he woke he didn't feel particularly refreshed. He had a shower and dressed. The thought suddenly struck him that he had no food in the flat, only coffee. He stood in front of the mirror, putting on his tie, and then glanced at his watch. By nature he was an early riser, and it was still only a little after eight. He supposed there would be somewhere he could get breakfast, London never slept, so it was said. He picked up his jacket. As he did so someone knocked on the front door. Who on earth could be calling at that time in the morning? Someone for Carol who didn't know she was dead? Mr X? No surely not. It couldn't be for himself, no one knew of his existence. There was only one way to find out. He undid the lock and pulled open the door.

Jackie stood in the hall, her face like a pale blossom in the dim light. He laughed, 'You gave me quite a fright, I wondered who on earth it could be.'

'I guessed you hadn't any food in the flat, I saw the light on when I got back last night and gathered you'd moved in. I hope I'm not intruding? I won't come in, but I'm just getting breakfast. I'll bring you a tray over in ten minutes.'

He had a sudden desperate longing for company, for the nearness of another human being. Tentatively he said, 'I could join you for breakfast.' She was like a breath of sanity, of security in what for some strange reason he felt was an alien world.

'I must say you are as welcome as the

flowers in May,' he grinned as she stood hesitating.

Then she said, 'OK. Come when you're ready.'

'I'm ready now, and starving!'

He followed her down the stairs. The mews was coming awake now, one or two people passed, but no one spoke either to him or Jackie. He hadn't taken very much notice of the flat on the other occasion he'd been inside. Now he saw one wall was covered with paintings and drawings, obviously done by children, matchstick men and animals, some flower studies. Some of them were really good. He stood with his hands on his hips, looking at them. They had obviously been executed with care and interest, the result of a good teacher, he thought. Somehow it was difficult to see Jackie in that role, she seemed such a quiet, gentle person, he couldn't imagine her having to deal with small children, who often could be noisy, naughty, even downright wicked, as he remembered himself and Carol sometimes. But perhaps, like Aunt Nora, Jackie didn't need to raise her voice, it was the very fact of her quiet, gentle personality that got through to them. Children were so much wiser than grown-ups in many ways.

He turned to the bookshelves. There were nothing like as many as in Carol's flat, most of the books were for children, or about them. A complete set of A. A. Milne's *Winnie the Pooh* and his poems. *Just So Stories* — he could imagine her surrounded by small children as she read in her soft voice. There was one shelf devoted to Devon, to Dartmoor, to the towns and villages. At heart was she a country girl?

Now he could smell the wonderful aroma of eggs and bacon coming from the tiny kitchen and wandered in to watch her. She moved deftly, gracefully, with a kind of neat economy that was delightful to watch. He leant against the sink, his arms folded.

'Don't mind me watching do you? I'm rather a plain cook myself, but always interested to see how others work.' He smiled at her. She threw back her hair with one hand, a gesture he had noticed before if she felt a little shy.

'I'm certainly no expert, but I get by. My Mum's the one. She and Dad keep a pub in Devon.' Aha he thought, so I was right . . .

'She's a super cook, they've built up quite a reputation in South Allington the village I come from. People even come from North Devon and Plymouth to eat her omelettes and lasagne. She's also a pizza expert, and of course pasties too with a secret recipe handed down for generations.'

Rob had seen a photograph of a young man in sweater and jeans in the living room, standing by a tractor; he didn't like to ask who he was at this juncture.

Now Jackie put the eggs and bacon on a plate with a piece of golden fried bread, a tomato and a couple of mushrooms, and handed it to him. 'Will that be enough? I'm not really used to cooking breakfast for . . . ' She broke off and her eyes swung away from him, the colour rising up her neck to her cheeks. He too turned away so she shouldn't feel embarrassed at the unfinished sentence.

'It looks like ambrosia fit for the gods. Are you going to join me?'

She shook her head, 'No, I just have fruit juice and toast. I never seem to have much time in the mornings. I like to sit and enjoy my food, eat it slowly. Mum always says I remind her of a contented calf chewing the cud!' She laughed now and Rob thought what a delightful sound it was. The first time he had heard it.

'What a description!'

'I know, but Mum's like that. You'd get on well I think.'

'What age are the children you teach?' He waved his hand at the pictures on the wall.

'Oh babies really, from about 5 to 6, sometimes a bit older, but mostly very young.'

'Do you enjoy it?'

Her face lit up, 'I love it.'

He mopped up the last of the bacon fat with a piece of bread. 'I can't remember when I enjoyed a meal more, 'specially breakfast.'

He looked at her once more and she smiled, 'I've never had breakfast with a stranger before,' the words tumbled out.

'I suppose it is looked upon as a rather intimate meal, but we are neighbours for a little while.'

She got up and took his plate, putting marmalade and toast in front of him. 'What are you going to do now? Stay in the flat, or have you to go back to South America at once?'

He spread marmalade. It was homemade and full of chunks of orange peel, just as he liked it, just as Nora used to make. Probably more of Jackie's Mum's cooking. He didn't look at her now as he said, 'I shall take a little holiday I think. They can manage without me for the time being. No one is indispensable.'

She glanced at her watch.

'Heavens, I must fly, or Miss Gilling will have me on toast, she hates unpunctuality. As a matter of fact, so do I.'

'What do you do for lunch, have it in the canteen?' he asked suddenly.

She picked up a bag from the kitchen chair and held it up. 'A snack, a couple of sandwiches, a Crunchie bar and some fruit. I eat it in the local park, opposite the school, in the fine weather like today.'

'Have lunch with me, a small thank you for breakfast,' he said impulsively.

She grinned again. It really was enchanting. 'What, and waste all this food?' She put on her jacket, 'Please just leave the dishes, I'll do them tonight.'

'Crunchie bars and some fruit aren't good,' he said quickly, 'please,' suddenly he was serious, 'I do need company right now.'

She looked at him. Her eyes were so

intensely blue it was as if pieces of summer sky had fallen into them. He pulled himself up sharply, he must be getting sentimental in his old age. Those kind of thoughts weren't like him at all.

Her voice was grave now, earnest as she said, 'I know. All right. I come out of school just after midday.' She took an old envelope from her bag and wrote down the address. 'You can get there by bus, it isn't far.'

'I might even walk,' he said. 'I'm used to being fairly active and I don't seem to have had much exercise lately.'

'You can cut through the park, it's lovely at this time of year. Think you can find it?'

'I'll plug in my radar, or ask a policeman,' he said. 'I'll be waiting for you.'

'Tell you what, you could call in the bakers on the corner of the mews and ask for some stale bread. They nearly always have some. We could feed the ducks. They usually expect something.'

'Fine.' He stood up and followed her to the door. She turned, 'Just drop the latch and bang it will you?'

Impulsively he took hold of her arm, catching a hint of her perfume. It was light, fresh as she was, reminding him of a country lane in summer, of honeysuckle and wild roses.

Suddenly, he couldn't tell why, he said slowly, 'Do you know any reason at all why Carol should have been afraid. Why she should *live in fear*?' He emphasised the last three words a little.

Her reply surprised him almost as much as his own question.

'Don't we all?' She pulled the door behind her as she went out.

5

The little flat seemed very lonely as her footsteps disappeared down the stairs to the mews outside. He went over to the window and watched her. She walked lightly with a spring in her step. 'I'll bet she's a good dancer,' he thought inconsequentially. Then, as if she felt his eyes on her, she turned, tossing back the long shining hair. Seeing him, she lifted her hand in a tiny gesture of greeting. He waved back. Then she was gone through the archway that led into the street.

He washed the dishes and tidied up, putting the dishes away. Everything was very neat with an almost childlike simplicity somehow.

He looked at his watch. It was only a little after nine. The next step was to go to the local 'nick'. 'Police' was the first of his sub-headings under 'London' on the schedule he had drawn up for himself. He wasn't sure where the station would be, but he supposed he could find it in the telephone directory or perhaps, as he had said to Jackie over her directions to the school, he could ask a policeman.

However neither necessity arose because as he turned into the main street, he saw, on the other side of the road, the brick building with a blue lamp outside with the word 'Police' painted on it.

He pushed open the swing door and went in. He couldn't remember ever having been inside a police station before. It was a pretty soulless place, the walls painted a sickly green, the smell of disinfectant and stale tobacco heavy on the air. Some rather sad looking rubber plants in tubs stood huddled in one corner like sheep that had been driven by a dog. Several people sat on benches against the wall, staring into space. He wondered what they waited for. He went up to the counter marked 'Enquries'. A young round-faced police constable asked him if he could help. He looked like a shoolboy to Rob. He thought, 'They're right, it's a sign of getting old; must be when you think how young the policemen look, and yet I'm only in my late twenties — '

The constable asked him his name, and what he wanted. 'I'm Robin Stanton I've come for my sister's car, Carol Stanton,' The man wrote down the information — 'Your address please sir?' This took some little while as he had to explain he was on leave from South America, the mews was only a temporary address.

'Have you no permanent address in England, sir?' The policeman scratched his ear. Rob was beginning to lose patience. 'Yes, no, well I have someone living up in the Midlands, she's not exactly a relation, but would that do? Not that I can see it has anything connected with the fact that all I want to do is take my sister's car.'

'Quite sir,' He wrote down Nora's address in Blisford. Rob had imagined this business over the car would be easy, that there would be some kind of standard arrangement, somewhere car keys were kept under these circumstances, that it would simply mean signing for the vehicle, identifying himself and being given the keys. It was the first time he'd really come up against British bureaucracy.

'Please take a seat.' The policeman referred to a list, running his finger down the entries. For a moment he glanced at Rob, then back at the list.

'I shan't keep you a moment, sir.'

Feeling more ruffled than ever, Rob took his place among the other people sitting in varying degrees of impatience along the benches that lined the walls. No one spoke. Normally he would probably have started up some kind of conversation with his fellow men and women, by nature he was an extrovert, but the gloomy atmosphere seemed to have seeped into his very bones.

He read the notices which were pasted on the wall. A warning About Rabies . . . a photokit picture of a man, underneath it said 'Have you seen this man?' A notice about dog licences, a police ball. He wished he'd brought a paper to read. How on earth did it take this long to find a set of keys? Perhaps they'd lost them . . . At that moment the constable returned.

'Chief Superintendent Crichton will see you now, sir.' Rob sensed a slight change in the constable's demeanour. It was as if some kind of shutter had come down, not that the man had been particularly friendly before, it was difficult exactly to put his finger on the change. It was as if Rob was now on the other side of some kind of fence — not just the relationship that usually pertained between the police and the man in the street — if he hadn't told himself it was ridiculous, he would have called it almost cagey, even antagonistic.

He was led down a dingy passage with echoing stone floor. They came to a door marked 'Chief Superintendent'. The constable knocked and a voice said, 'Come in, please.'

The man in the dark blue uniform with the silver badges of rank on his shoulders sat with his back to the light. Rob couldn't tell if he was young or old, dark of fair. The sun shone through the window behind him, temporarily blinding Rob. He wondered if this was intentional to intimidate criminals. He also wondered why on earth such a high ranking officer should trouble to see him about so small a matter as picking up a car. However he did feel a sense of gratitude too, that the police should care enough about the situation to do so.

'Please sit down, Mr Stanton. Constable Green, bring some coffee will you?'

He held out his hand to Rob, 'My name is Crichton, Chief Superintendent Crichton.' Rob sat in the chair he had indicated. The man's handshake had been firm and warm. He felt some of his faith in the system returning. At last perhaps he was getting somewhere, here was someone he would be able to talk to.

The superintendent held out a packet of cigarettes, flicked his lighter and Rob drew the comforting nicotine deep into his lungs. Waiting outside, his nerves had started to jangle. Now he felt reassured.

'I am so sorry you are here on such a sad errand, Mr Stanton. Suicide of a loved one is a most upsetting business. Very hard on those left, the next of kin, which I understand is your position with regard to the late Miss Carol Stanton?'

Rob nodded, 'Yes, and thank you for your sympathy, Superintendent, but quite frankly it is simply beyond my comprehension why she should have done it. There was no reason, she wasn't that kind of girl, the last person you could possibly think of doing such a thing. We grew up together, shared our lives well into our teens. There can't be anyone who knew Carol better than I did. It's just beyond belief. I still can't accept the fact.'

The superintendent poured coffee from the earthenware pot which had been brought, with cream and sugar and a plate of fancy biscuits. Slowly he said, 'How long was it since you had seen your sister, Mr Stanton?'

'Oh some months, more than that perhaps. Where I live and work one rather loses count of time passing. I suppose perhaps a year, eighteen months. But she wrote often. I'm afraid I didn't always reply. I'm not much of a letter writer, but her letters were typical, full of the joy of life, of humour. She was a complete extrovert, and surely extroverts, with everything going for them, don't end it all.' He ground out the cigarette in the ashtray.

'Quite, I understand exactly how you feel, but you know such a lot can happen to the young, in such a short time. They are impressionable, vulnerable. People change. 'Specially it seems these days. Values are not what they were. When I was young for instance, family life meant more . . . and there doesn't seem to be the responsibility, the caring there used to be.' For a moment Rob wondered if he meant this as some kind of criticism of himself, but he went on, 'We don't really know what does worry some people, things that others can shrug off. In fact, do we really know another human being, however long we may live with them? I doubt it.'

'I suppose you're right, and I was hundreds of miles away, I admit.'

As Rob spoke, the superintendent got up and went over to the window. It looked out on a small yard with a square of grass in the middle, soot laden, scratched by visiting cats from the neighbouring houses. A pigeon stood there now, cleaning its feathers. 'Depression, overwork, so many things can change the personality. I have seen it so many times, perhaps an unfortunate love affair. For some it is easy to flit from one to another, transient, forgetting; with some it goes deep, a wound that cannot be healed if that love is lost.'

Rob was amazed that this man should speak so fully, that he was so deep thinking. He had never somehow connected a policeman with this kind of insight and compassion. For a moment he thought of mentioning the coded note he had found in the book of poems, but at once he dismissed it. There was no reason he would be able to help, to explain. After all, Carol's death had been an isolated incident on their patch no more than that. They probably had dozens of suicides, murders, violence and mugging every week from what he read in the papers.

Crichton came back from the window now, sat down and drained the rest of the coffee.

'Now Mr Stanton, to be practical, is there anything we can do for you?'

Rob put down his empty cup. 'Yes. I really came in about my sister's car.'

It so happened that he was looking directly at Crichton as he said the words. For a moment an expression which he could only describe as, wary, flashed across the man's face. It was immediately replaced with blandness once more. Rob wondered if he had imagined it. The look had been cagey, touching his eyes, his mouth. No, it couldn't be. He was letting his imagination get the better of him. He could hear Nora telling him so, 'Fancies, love, just fancies.'

Crichton got up abruptly again, almost upsetting his chair. 'The car? Oh yes of course. We must see about returning it to you.'

'Returning it? But I'd like to take it now, fill in the necessary forms or whatever, sign for it.'

The superintendent gave a tight smile, which did nothing for his eyes. 'Ah, now you have touched on the vital spot, Mr Stanton. Formalities and forms. You see it is very difficult under these circumstances; the licence, the

71

insurance, all in your sister's name. If she made it over to you, of course it would be different. But in this case . . . '

Rob was beginning now to feel the return of the irritation he had felt as he waited outside. But perhaps the man was right. The wheels of insurers, licence offices, did turn slowly, he knew that.

'Oh yes I see, I suppose I can wait.' A sudden idea struck him. It might sound heartless, but he would have to risk that. 'The only thing is, I am staying in England for a little while. I shall want to go up to the Midlands to see my aunt, and with transport so expensive, I was hoping to be able to transfer the car to my name, and to use it, you see.'

For a moment again the impassive mask slipped as Crichton said almost sharply now, 'I'm sorry, Mr Stanton. It is quite impossible to arrange it just in a day like that. We shall have to put the wheels in motion and let you know.' He had got to his feet. Rob felt he was being dismissed. Somehow the superintendent had come to the end of his patience, or whatever. Was it that? Or something more.

'I see. Well thank you for your time and interest, Superintendent.'

He stepped out into the sunshine, his mind in a whirl like a ferris wheel. Why on earth could they not let him have it back? What possible use had they for it now, weeks after the whole business had been cleared up and closed? The inquest itself over and finished. Finalised.

He remembered Carol's little Mini. It was one of those cheeky City models, painted a bright yellow, sunshine yellow, when she had bought it. She wrote and told him she had added the stencil of a huge marigold on the bonnet, 'Like the one Danny Kaye used to sing about in the inch worm song, remember? It's got a happy look somehow, makes the lorry drivers laugh when I'm stuck in one of those endless queues in town.'

He'd go and look in the police pound. The cars stood in serried ranks, shimmering in the hot sun. A Rolls, a Jag, a Merc — some bent and smashed, some pristine in their perfection. Minis, Fords, pick-ups and station wagons. But although he walked along the rows, there was no sign of a yellow Mini. A small finger of fear, an icy chill ran up his spine.

'If it's not here,' he thought, 'then where the hell is it?'

6

He glanced at his watch. It was eleven o'clock. An hour until Jackie had said she would be free.

He'd get some sandwiches from a takeaway, collect some stale bread for the ducks as she had suggested. God, he needed someone to talk to, some sane, rational company. He felt more and more as if he were wrapped in a fog, fighting against something intangible, impenetrable. Now and then it was as if some kind of clue, some piece of information was in his grasp and then, as he put out his hand to take it, like an eel, it slipped away, grinning over its shoulder in derision. And yet why should he feel like this? Who were these nebulous enemies he kept imagining?

He crossed the park and walked down a tree-shaded road. There was the red brick school, it must have been a pre-war building, or even older, it had a kind of mellow grace about it. There were tubs of flowers in the playground, pictures stuck up in the windows like the drawings and paintings he had seen in Jackie's flat. Somehow, in spite of the fact that she was quiet, a shy person, he felt the stamp of her personality had imprinted itself even here in the classrooms, which he could only glimpse through the windows.

A bell rang, and suddenly a wave of children poured out, tumbling, scrapping, laughing and shouting like small animals. And there she was, among them. She stopped to tie a shoelace, to pat a small head, to blow someone's nose, to bend down and laugh at a child who held something out to her. Then she saw him. She stood for a moment, a little uncertain, then she smiled, tossed back her hair, and came towards him.

'Hi neighbour!' she grinned, as he hailed her.

The sun was really hot and the grass

and trees looked cool and inviting in the park. She led him to a seat near the lake, which curved away into the distance, under a bridge. The water shimmered in the summer sun, and ducks of every kind swam and dived, their tails sticking out of the water as they upended after some tasty morsels. She started to laugh and, in a few seconds, she was rolling about like a small, uncontrolled child. It was delightful to watch such joy, and infectious too, so that he joined in and was laughing as he hadn't done for months.

At last she stopped and wiped the tears from her eyes.

Smiling he said, 'Now, perhaps you could tell me what that was about!'

'It's the ducks.' She had difficulty in speaking, the laughing had turned to hiccups. 'I once read somewhere, when God had made the first duck he laughed, and I'm not surprised . . . I think they are quite the funniest things I have ever seen and it's just that, like some comedians who do the same for me, I have to laugh whenever I see them.'

'I hadn't thought of it before, but you're right.'

'Well then, what were you laughing at?' she teased.

'At you — laughing!'

'Oh my goodness!' Once more she started, then she said, 'At home we used to have a couple of Muscovy ducks. They really are the most comic of all, you know, they bow their heads at each other all the time. These were pure white with round, blue eyes. They used to waddle along side by side, the duck leading, the drake following. Honestly, you could tell they were a married couple.'

Now they threw the stale bread, watching the ducks for a little while. Suddenly she turned to him. 'What did you mean by that question this morning? Whether I had any idea why Carol should have been afraid, lived in fear?'

He was silent for a moment, then he said, 'Perhaps you think I'm a bit nutty, that the whole thing has turned my brain, but I simply cannot accept the idea that Carol committed suicide. I have to have some logical explanation of why she did it, why she was so unhappy, changed so much, that she could even contemplate such a thing. I have to find out what, or who, made her so desperate. You see she wrote marvellous letters, full of the kind of humour and gaiety we've just experienced over those ducks. Right up to the last one I received.' He hesitated a moment, but he knew he had to say it, had to tell her. 'Another thing, it seems a bit ridiculous now as I talk about it, but last night when I went into her bedroom, even her nightie was neatly folded on the bed. Someone who intends to kill themselves doesn't do that. It just doesn't make sense. Her eyes were on his face whilst he spoke. Now he took the piece of paper from his wallet on which he had written the code, and the words he had worked out. 'I live with fear . . . ' Briefly he explained it to her, and said, 'Can you explain to me, rationalise, why she should have written that? A perfectly normal, healthy, ordinary girl? It just doesn't make sense.'

She didn't answer for a moment, then she said, 'Look, if you analyse it, there are lots of different interpretations you could put on it. Perhaps she was ill, or thought she was. Perhaps she really was having this affair they talked about, and was afraid of it being found out at the office. Or, if she was the kind of person I think she was — both from what you have told me, and the brief encounters I had with her — maybe she cared deeply about the terrible things that go on in the world today. Heaven knows it's enough to make one think is it all worth it? Even I have sometimes.' She glanced away, then went on, 'The balance of power they are always talking about, nuclear war, bombs, terror, mugging, little children being destroyed, mutilated. If you do think about it it can prey on your mind and become almost too much.' She stopped again, he was going to say something, when she said, 'On the other hand have you thought it might be a joke she shared with someone else, someone she had tried to explain to about your code as kids? Or even be a message left over from that time that you had forgotten about.'

He shook his head slowly, wanting to believe, but not able to. He crumbled some of the remaining stale bread in his fingers, throwing it to the ducks.

'I know all you say is rational, feasible, but it just won't wash. It simply doesn't tie in with the Carol I knew. I still say, if she did kill herself, then someone drove her to it. And another thing, I've just been to the local copshop about her car, asked if I could have it. I saw the top brass. There's no joy, just a long and complicated explanation which added up to nothing, but meant I couldn't have it. I had a look in the pound, it wasn't there. Why wasn't it?'

She shrugged her shoulders. 'There could be a logical explanation. Perhaps they have some kind of special lock-up for cars that are termed 'evidence' . . . ' She glanced at him quickly, hoping she hadn't hurt him, reminded him painfully, but he was gazing at the lake. 'Maybe they have special bays somewhere, under cover, where they can go over a car carefully; you know, if they've been stolen or used in raids or anything like that, they go over them for fingerprints.'

'But why should they go over a car where a suicide has occurred for fingerprints? And if it is somewhere special, then why not say so? What's all the mystery about?'

Slowly she said, her eyes on his face, 'Are you trying to tell me something?'

'Yes. At least I'm telling myself something through you. Thinking out loud. Things aren't adding up. Something isn't right. I can feel it in my bones. And I don't like it.'

'You see it's terribly difficult for me to judge, to help. I didn't know her terribly well. Of course we used to meet in the mews sometimes, I borrowed some sugar from her once, she brought over a letter which had been delivered at her place by mistake. The kind of thing neighbours do.' She stopped for a moment as if she had just remembered something. He turned and looked at her.

'Yes?'

'Well there was a time, not so long ago actually, I'd almost forgotten. She came over one evening, just after I'd got back from school. When I opened the door she just stood there for a moment, as if she was bewildered, didn't quite know where she was, almost as if she didn't really know why she had come. There was a vague, distant look in her eyes. Confused. And I thought she didn't look well. It was difficult to explain. She was pale, thin, it's silly really, but it was as if she'd suddenly aged, or as if she was haunted by something.' Jackie stopped again and looked up at him under her lashes. 'Does that sound ridiculous?'

'No, under the circumstances, not at all. I suppose it's what I've been waiting for someone to tell me, what I half-expected. Go on, what happened then?' He sounded almost brusque in his anxiety.

'Nothing, that's just it. She came in and sat down. Then she said, 'Have you got an egg to spare? I seem to have run out'. It was so obviously untrue, I almost laughed. I couldn't imagine what possible reason she could have to so blatantly manufacture an excuse. After, I did wonder if it could be a need for company in some way, a kind of call for help, but I dismissed the whole idea as ridiculous. I was sure she had lots of friends, although I thought about it after, and it did seem less and less people came to the flat. At one time she used to have quite a crowd at weekends. As a matter of fact I felt quite flattered that she'd come. I gave her some eggs, and she got up. She seemed a bit reluctant to go. I asked her to stay and join me for supper. At first I did think she was going to say yes, but it was as if she suddenly thought of something. She said, 'No, thanks all the same. I have an appointment. Thanks for the eggs. I'll replace them tomorrow'. And that was all.'

'Did you talk at all?'

'Not really. It was hard going, which was most unusual from what I knew of Carol. She just sat on the sofa and talked a bit, but really she didn't say anything much. Do you know what I mean?'

'I think so.'

'I asked her if she was OK. She said she had a bit of a problem, but she guessed it would work out. I asked her if a man was involved, although I didn't want to seem to be probing. It really wasn't any of my business.'

'And what did she say to that?' He

leant forward now, hanging on her reply.

'She tried to smile, but not very successfully, and said, 'Isn't there always?' It was a very odd meeting. It really quite upset me at the time, but I didn't want to intrude. I wished after that I had because I never saw her again. I have an awful feeling now, with the way you talk, that it could have been some kind of cry for help which I was too thick to see.'

He shook his head, 'I doubt if you or anyone could have helped, you have nothing to blame yourself with, and thank you for telling me.'

She got up and shook the crumbs from her skirt. 'I must get back.'

Suddenly he took her hands in his. 'What do you live in fear of, Jackie?'

She glanced at him, her eyes puzzled.

'Don't you remember what you said to me this morning when I asked you why Carol should live in fear, and you said, 'Don't we all?' She pulled her hand away, dropping her gaze,

7

He was thankful that at least he now had something to do, something tangible. He leafed through the yellow pages of the phone book and found a garage nearby who hired out cars. He was shocked at the price he had to pay, but he chose a nearly new, powerful model, he was looking forward to driving on a motorway after the dirt roads he was used to. Then he went to a supermarket to buy some groceries. If he was going to stay in the flat for some time, he had better stock up and there was the next day's breakfast he had promised Jackie.

When he got back to the flat and had to open the garage door to put the car away, once more he felt a coldness along his nerves, but the flat was cheerful in the afternoon sun and he made himself a meal. When he finished he brewed a big pot of coffee, and settled down once more with his 'work plan'.

He looked at the headings. He hadn't got very far, but at least he'd been to the police, although that had turned out to be a dead end, unsatisfactory in every way. He added a note 'Return to pick up car. Insist on having it or want to know why'. He had also managed to talk to Jackie a little about Carol, and about the last time she had seen her — which actually had added to his feeling of unease. He added all that to the notes. He wanted to think now, mull over what she had said. Some music would help him to concentrate, it always did. He went over to the music centre. Somehow he couldn't face up to using the record player yet, with the Vivalidi still on it. He switched on the tape section. He'd chosen a tape of Chopin studies labelled in Carol's handwriting. She must have recorded them from a concert on the radio he supposed.

The lovely delicate notes of the first piece, the Nocturne No 15 in F Minor — a chanson triste — filled the room. For a moment he listened, without moving, to the wistful little phrase which occurred again and again, gaining significance with every recurrence. It was followed by the Scherzo No 1 in B Minor, with an angry tornado of sound mounting up to a terrific climax. He had gone back to his notes now. Tomorrow he would see Nora. His pencil moved to the heading of 'NORTH' He'd go along and see this chap, Frank Barton. As he underlined the name he remembered how Jackie had told him Carol's reply when she asked her if there was a man behind her problem — 'Isn't there always?' Yes, indeed he'd have a word with Mr Barton . . .

Suddenly he realised the music had stopped, but the tape was still running. A sound came from the twin speakers which hit him like a hammer blow. It was so achingly familiar, the voice, and yet so bizarre in its strangeness.

It was Carol's voice all right, but she was talking what sounded like gibberish. A foreign language which he didn't understand, didn't recognise. For some reason the hair on the back of his neck felt as if it was rising like a dog's hackles.

He leapt to his feet and switched off the recorder. He felt a chill all over as if someone had blown an icy blast into the flat. He wrenched open the door, tore down the stairs, hardly conscious of what he did, across the narrow mews to Jackie's flat, and hammered on the door. There was no reply.

Reaction was a feeling of foolishness, and a relief she wasn't in. He was behaving like an hysterical schoolgirl.

Slowly he went back to his own flat. He couldn't settle now to anything. He kept going over to the tape deck and staring down at it as if it could answer all the questions thronging his mind. Then he wandered over to the window. It was getting late now, evening. People hurried about their business, making him feel more lonely than ever. If only Jackie would come . . .

After what seemed hours, he heard footsteps along the hallway outside. He opened the door and called to her.

'What's the matter? You look as if something terrible has happened. As if you'd seen a ghost . . . ' She bit her lips directly she had spoken. It was tactless in the extreme, but his appearance had thrown her, really shocked her.

Without answering her question, he said, 'Listen to this.' He switched on the tape, then stood watching her face. He hadn't even asked her to sit down. She looked at him, her eyes puzzled.

'Well?' he said with some impatience. 'What do you make of that? It is Carol, isn't it?'

She nodded, 'Yes, yes it's Carol's voice all right.'

'But what about the words, what she is saying, the language. It sounds like gibberish.'

Jackie had to smile in spite of his

serious expression and obvious emotion.

'It's Russian. She's just saying 'Can
you help me? I'd like cream in my
coffee, and sugar, please.' I expect she
was doing a course in Russian and that
was part of her homework.'

'But why?' he shot the remark at her
like the bullet from a gun.

'Why not? I did the same. There were
at least a dozen other people at the
evening class I went to. People of all
ages.'

'But why, why, *why*?' The words were
out before he thought. Once more her
calmness and reason made him feel he
was overeacting, an unreasonable impatience with both himself and her. He
tried to return to normality, switching
off the recorder, telling her to sit down
and he'd get her a drink.

'I'd love a lager if you've got one, I've
been to the Parent/Teachers' evening,
and they really are a bit exhausting.
Everyone seems to talk *at* you somehow, and of course they want to know

all the details about their own child, which figures, but it's a bit wearing.' She took the lager from him gratefully, the glass frosty with the cold liquid from the fridge. She drained the glass and then got to her feet.

'If we're off on the razzle dazzle tomorrow, I must really get a bit of work done. Thanks so much, you saved my life.'

As she reached the door, he said, 'Why did you learn Russian? Surely you don't need it in your job?'

She turned round slowly, grinning, 'No, but when I was studying I needed an extra O-level, I wanted to do something different, and a bit exciting. I'd even planned I might go on a trip to Moscow one day. OK?'

He went towards her, trying now to smile at the normality, the perfectly rational explanation she had once again given. Impulsively he bent and kissed her cheek. 'OK, teacher!'

When she had gone he listened to the tape two or three times, trying to assess the tone of Carol's voice, but it still sounded like gibberish to him. At last he went to bed and fell asleep almost immediately.

He woke, drenched in sweat, just as if he had been standing in the rain. For a moment he had no idea where he was. Something terrible had happened, he was sure of it. He looked at his luminous watch. Three-thirty. He sat up and switched on the light, gazing round the room. He was wide awake now. It had been a nightmare he supposed, but so vivid it still haunted him. He sniffed. His nostrils were filled with a most peculiar smell. For a moment he didn't recognise it. Then he realised it was car exhaust. Carbon monoxide. He heard an engine running somewhere outside. Now his nightmare came back to him in detail. He had seen Carol in her car, in the garage. He knew she was suffocating, her hands stretched out towards him in supplication. Desperately he tried to open the door, to get to her, but his limbs were paralysed. He couldn't lift a finger to help her. He tried to shout, but no sound came.

He got out of bed and went to the window, lifting the curtain. In the mews below some people had obviously just returned from a party, a very merry one by the look of it. Voices shouted, laughed, doors banged, eventually the car drove off. It must have been the fumes from it beneath his window that he had smelt.

Back in bed he lighted a cigarette. He was wide awake now, the sweat clammy on his body. Silence had fallen over the mews. He could only hear the distant hum of traffic in the heart of the city that never slept.

He listened to the sound of his own heart beating.

Everything now that had happened since he came to England whirled through his mind like speeded up film, all the moments stored away in his subconscious, details that had puzzled him, things he had tried to rationalise away. The verdict of suicide, the Mr X affair, the way he had been fobbed off by the superintendent, the coded message, the folded nightgown . . . Jackie's remarks on how Carol had looked that last time she had seen her.

Frank Barton.

The change that even Nora had noticed from so far away. And now the talk in Russian.

Individually he supposed they were all acceptable, feasible. Put together, there in the darkness, they added up to the unacceptable. He stubbed out his cigarette. Was he over-acting? Was he being hysterical? No, he was absolutely convinced something was going on . . . had gone on. He turned out the light. He heard a distant clock strike the quarters until four o'clock, then at last he fell into a fitful sleep . . . hearing her voice . . .

8

He woke with a start to feel the warm sun on his face, shining through the window where he had left the curtains undrawn. He glanced at his watch. It was already after seven, and he had told Jackie to be over promptly at eight for breakfast.

He showered and put on a short-sleeved tee shirt and denims. From the clarity of the sky, and the shimmer of heat already rising from the roof of the mews opposite, it was going to be a perfect July day. He was glad the car he had hired had a sunshine roof. They could drive with the fresh air and sunshine around them instead of being shut inside a mechanical box. He had grown so used to being out of doors, that when he had to spend any time within four walls, he felt restricted, almost a feeling of claustrophobia.

He put the frying pan on the stove and laid strips of fresh bacon in it, cut slices of brown bread and popped them under the grill; the coffee was already percolating and gradually the wonderful smell of frying, mixed with the aromas of coffee and toast, filled the little flat.

Her knock was gentle, and dead on time.

'Gosh, I could smell the breakfast half across the mews. I wonder why food, and the thought thereof is always so much more appetising when you've had nothing to do with it yourself?'

He grinned, 'I only hope the anticipation isn't going to be better than the realisation, I'm a bit out of practise.' His eyes took in the charming picture she made, like a summer morning itself, he thought, in a yellow shirt and scarlet dungarees. He lifted an eyebrow in mock astonishment, 'I thought you were the plumber for a moment!'

She looked down at the rather workmanlike clothes and said quickly,

'Sorry, will it be OK? I hate dressing up in my time off, I have to do a certain amount for my job, it's so nice to relax.'

'Of course, I was only teasing. You look delicious and just right for our trip.'

By quarter to nine they had washed the dishes and were in the car. He drove slowly through the traffic until he reached the Motorway. 'I expect I seem an old dodderer to you who are used to London traffic, but we don't see many vehicles where I've been working, mostly mules and llamas, and although they may create some problems, they are hardly the cause of traffic jams!'

She smiled at him, 'I like driving slowly, it gives me a chance to see all that's going on. I have a very curious nature, like the elephant's child, an insatiable curiosity.'

'Good.' He switched on the radio and she started to sing to the music, her voice sweet and melodious. It seemed in no time at all they were running past Birmingham, 'No wonder they call this spaghetti junction,' he said, 'it's like a maze, bit of luck we didn't end up in Wales, I nearly missed the turning.' They were on a secondary road now, and gradually this gave way to smaller roads. They passed through a couple of villages, and then saw the sign to Blisford. As they drew nearer he pointed out familiar landmarks.

'Oddly enough it hasn't changed all that much, not this part. I suppose there's nothing for the tycoons to spread their horrible tentacles for, no holiday attractions, so parts of it are still unspoilt. See that stream in the meadow? That's where I once caught a swallow on my fishing line, I'll never forget it. I was casting, and as I let the rod back over my shoulder, a bird seized the fly on the wing. It was ghastly. The line ran out as it struggled, but Carol and I managed to catch the bird and get the hook out of its beak. It flew off, apparently none the worse, but that put an end to my fishing days.'

'You had fun as kids, being two of

you,' she sounded a little wistful, 'I was a spoilt only . . . '

'Yes we did, once Nora took us under her wing; things hadn't been too good before that.'

She was silent for a moment, then said softly, 'I do hope she's going to like me.'

He took her hand and squeezed it. 'No fear of her not doing so, I promise you.'

Now he turned in through a farm gate and up a rutted drive. Although it was untidy, it was far from neglected. Hens and geese, some cows and a goat were roaming the fields which ran either side of the road. Two donkeys trotted up to the fence as they saw them go by. They drew up in the yard which flanked the front of the low, stone house, hardly more than a cottage. A small girl was feeding some hens, scattering the corn whilst a sheepdog lay in the sun, watching. Two cats cleaned themselves on a low wall. It was like a scene from the past in its tranquillity, and the rosy-cheeked plump woman who came from the open doorway, wiping her hands on her apron, fitted perfectly into the background.

Rob jumped out and enfolded Nora in his arms. She hugged him close, 'It's good to see you, love. And of you to come so soon. I was afraid once you got down in that old city, you'd never find the time.'

'It's only a flying visit, but I had to come,' he said, turning round as Jackie got slowly out of the car, not sure yet what her reception would be. She knew how much Nora and Rob meant to each other, he had never stopped talking of her on the way up. But Nora came towards her with outstretched arms.

'Welcome my dear. I am so glad you came with Rob. He told me on the phone he would bring you. Come along in, you must be starving, and dying to wash. These long car journeys make you feel like a smut, I know.'

Rob had to laugh, 'Honestly, Nora, you're going back to the days of the horseless carriage. Just because you never leave home, you don't know how the world has progressed. It's only taken just over a couple of hours and we still feel fresh as daisies. Although I have to admit my breakfast does seem to have disappeared.'

Jackie laughed, 'It was jolly good though. I can recommend him as a cook.'

Nora led them into the cottage, 'You don't mind coming to the kitchen do you, love? We never seem to get around to using the front door. I suppose we should, but we seem to gravitate to the kitchen, the heart of the house, where everything seems to happen.'

The room was stone-flagged, low-ceilinged, typical of a small farmhouse. Most of the land had been split up from the original, Rob had told her, Nora kept a couple of fields for her miscellany of animals.

A wonderful smell came from the

solid fuel cooker, the table was laid with a blue and white check cloth with honey-coloured pottery plates and cups and saucers. Rob glanced round and sighed contentedly.

'Nothing's changed, thank God. It's almost magic. Sometimes, alone there on the altiplano, I think about this place, remember where everything stands.' He waved at the dresser with its clutter of china, a workbasket with some mending spilling from it, old magazines, books, and a china vase with paper flowers, a small palm cross from Easter Sunday long ago. It had a permanence, a feeling of the past like an aura about it.

Nora was busy at the oven, dishing up an enormous piece of beef, turning out a crisp, golden Yorkshire pudding, stirring the meat tin of rich gravy. Jackie gave an appreciative sniff.

'I feel just like a Bisto kid. I never smelt anything so marvellous.'

'Where are the rest of the family?' Rob asked at last.

'They've all gone to the fair in Blisford, except for Annie. You probably saw her outside, feeding the hens. She doesn't like what she calls 'they roundabouts and them dogem cars,' so she decided to stay and help me, but don't worry, they'll all be back later, we never stay quiet for long.'

They ate with slow enjoyment and already Jackie felt, from the way Nora treated her and the welcome she had received, as if she was one of the family. The beef was accompanied by roast potatoes, fresh beans from the garden, parsnips, carrots, leeks, horseradish sauce, and to follow apple tart liberally covered with cream.

Jackie said at last, 'I shall have to go for a brisk walk after this feast.' She and Nora grinned at each other, and Rob said, 'The way to a man's heart may be through his stomach, but the way to Nora's is to tell her you like her cooking!'

She gave him a gentle slap, 'Rubbish. I've been at it too long to take notice, long as people enjoy their food.' She glanced at Annie who was a pale, quiet little girl. She had hidden behind the door when she heard Jackie and Rob with Nora, and the latter had had to lift her up and bring her in to meet them. But when Jackie bent to kiss her, she had lifted her face, and for a moment a smile had touched her lips. But she hadn't joined in the conversation, although she had methodically eaten the food put in front of her.

Rob knew there would be some kind of story behind her presence, sure to be if Nora had taken her under her wing. For a moment his mind flew back down the years to the time when he and Carol had been much like the small, pale Annie, until they had warmed themselves at Nora's generous fire.

She had picked a great bunch of summer flowers, roses, pinks, marigolds, and arranged them in a bouquet.

'I knew you'd want to go along to the church, love. Take these for her grave. You'd like to be alone, I expect.'

'Jackie would like to come. She would have liked to come to the funeral, but of course she didn't know where or when it was.'

Nora nodded, 'No she wouldn't. It was only in the local paper, and of course I didn't know the little maid's address.' She turned to Jackie and put her arm round her, 'Pity you didn't know her better. You two would have been friends.' Over her head she signalled her approval to Rob, and he grinned back mouthing the words, 'I knew you'd like her.'

'Oh by the way, where's this chap's garage, Frank Barton? I think I'll go and have a chat.' He hadn't told Nora it was one of his chief reasons from coming up to Blisford, apart from the joy of seeing her and his old home again.

'It's down where the old smithy used to be, remember? There's a ford over the stream near the bridge. Frank's grandfather was blacksmith one time; used to keep geese as watchdogs. One

109

of them had you by the pants once.' She burst out laughing, 'Old Hissock, you used to call him. Any road, that's Frank's garage now.' She paused a moment and put the flowers in Jackie's arms.

'There's no headstone yet,' she turned to Rob, 'we got to think about that, now you're here.'

It was no distance to the little church, approached by a long path edged with yew trees, some confetti still lay where it had been thrown for a recent wedding.

Jackie gave a little sigh, 'What a marvellous place to be married . . . I . . . ' she broke off as if she had changed her mind about finishing the sentence. Sensing there was something private, not to be shared at the moment, he didn't press her.

They found the grave, covered with flowers which Rob guessed were kept fresh by Nora. He stood for a moment, looking down at the grassy mound, His mind was winging back over the years

— Christmas Morning in the little stone church, the smell of paraffin, and evergreens, the lamplight on the scarlet holly berries. Summer evenings when the church door stood open and all the sounds of the country crowded in — the lowing of cows, the call of the wood pigeons, a dog barking, a shire horse calling to its foal . . . and the sound of voices singing.

At least now she lay at peace, the secret of her death buried with her. But not for long; he was determined to find out the truth, however long it might take. Jackie's hand crept into his, her fingers curling gently round his own, and the warmth brought him a measure of comfort, of assurance.

9

The stream chattered cheerfully over the stones, the water crystal clear. 'Used to be the leat that turned the mill wheel,' Rob said, pausing for a moment on the old stone bridge above the ford where he and Carol had fed the ducks and geese. Now there was only a pair of mallards, busy in the reeds with some young ones.

Two petrol pumps and a brick building stood where the forge had once been. There was the sound of hammering, and the smell of oil hung heavily on the warm summer afternoon.

'I'll wait for you on the bridge,' Jackie said, 'in fact I shouldn't wonder if I fall asleep after that wonderful meal, and the peaceful atmosphere. There's a seat under that tree there.'

The workshop was neat with all the tools arrayed tidily on racks. New tyres stood against one wall, two cars were in the process of having their engines repaired. Bright flowers in green tubs stood in the forecourt, there was a small shop which sold road maps, sweets and paperback books. Rob shouted, but there was no reply, then he saw a pair of feet protruding from under one of the cars in the workshop. He walked towards it and a young man appeared from underneath.

'Sorry sir, didn't hear you. Bit of trouble here with the back axle. Can I help you?' He was wiping his hands on a piece of cloth. For a moment Rob stood looking at him, sizing him up.

He was good-looking in a fresh, country style. Fair-haired, round-faced with blue eyes. There was a kind of boyish innocence about him so that he seemed hardly old enough to own a business, but Rob remembered Nora had said he had worked hard and deserved his success.

'Are you Frank Barton?' The question was direct, unequivocal. From the questioning expression on his face, it was obvious Frank was puzzled, even a little upset from the approach, the curt tone of voice.

'I am.'

'And were you Carol Stanton's boyfriend? How well did you know her? How long ago was it you last saw her, and what kind of a relationship did you have?'

Frank put the rag down carefully on the workbench before he replied, then he said, 'Hang about a bit, mate. Who's asking?'

'I'm her brother.'

'I see. Well in that case perhaps we'd better go into the office where we shan't be disturbed.' He turned towards the small shop, Rob followed. There was a desk, a typewriter and telephone, some files, all neatly arranged. He pulled out a chair and sat opposite Rob, behind the desk.

'Well, what is it you want to know exactly. I can't imagine there's much information you haven't already got.'

'They say Carol committed suicide while the balance of her mind was disturbed.' Rob's voice hardened now as he looked directly at Frank. 'What I'd like to know is did *you* do anything to disturb the balance of her mind, to upset her or cause her death?'

Frank had been sitting quietly, but now he exploded into wrath, leaping to his feet and knocking the telephone off the desk.

'Now look here, mate. I've work to do here, I run my own business, and mind my own business too in every sense of the word. I don't know what the hell your game is. I've given a full statement to the police, helped them in every way I can. I don't have to answer you. Go and ask them.'

Once again Rob felt this man knew more than he was saying. It must be a conspiracy, everyone he turned to kept him in ignorance about everything, every way he tried to turn he came up against a blank wall. Suddenly all the accumulated frustration and anger rose inside him. He jumped to his feet as a kind of scarlet wave of fury swept over him, fanned by his grief. He grabbed Frank by the front of his overalls and slammed him against the wall of the office before the other realised what was happening.

'What the hell happened to her? I have to know, God — I have to know!' Now for the first time, Frank looked directly into his eyes, trying to push him away. He saw anger, the ferocity of this man, but too he saw anguish, tears. He sagged in Rob's grasp and said gently, all his own anger spent, 'You tell me . . . you tell me mate.'

Rob let him go.

'Look, I'm going to make some coffee. I think we both need it. Then we'll talk.' As Frank spoke, Rob looked out of the window. He could see Jackie through the window, the slight breeze had ruffled her hair. She looked so sane, so placid. He turned to Frank who was stirring two coffee cups.

'Sugar? Milk?'

Rob nodded to both queries. Once more they sat down either side of the desk. Slowly at last Frank started to speak.

'Yes, I went around with Carol. Actually I was away at school when you two were at Nora's. Dad used to talk about you sometimes. I saw her once or twice in the distance. I thought she was terrific. It was quite a crush I had, but somehow I never got around to meeting you then. I suppose we moved in different circles, you living some little way out of the village, me going to school in the town.' He paused and sipped his coffee.

'Then we started dating. I took her seriously all right. She was that kind of girl. I don't mean she was serious, but she was the kind of girl you have a straight relationship with, no mucking about. Know what I mean?'

'We had some marvellous times together, although it was only a relatively short period we knew each other. We did a bit of riding, I used to let her drive my car. She loved driving. Then she got the little Mini. I gave it the onceover for her to make sure it was OK. What I loved about her was her laughter. She was always laughing, easy going. Such a lovely nature. Never be another like her, guess they broke the mould when she was made.' He paused a moment. Rob said with a touch of impatience.

'Go on.'

'Well then she changed. She became more thoughtful, quiet, almost glum you could say. She started to come up here less and less. I knew Nora was worried. Once or twice I tried to phone her at work during the day, but she was always 'out of the office.' If I rang her home number I got the engaged signal, till I began to think she had left it off the hook. I thought there must be someone else and it was the gentle brush off, trying not to hurt me, she was that kind of girl. Then one weekend not long ago, I couldn't stand not knowing any longer, even if the news was bad, I had to know. I made up my mind to ask her to get engaged, to think about marriage. I've got a nice little business here, it's all my own, no mortgage. There's no competition in the area, and people need cars more and more in the country. I felt I had something really good to offer.'

He got up and went over to the window. Rob was impatient for him to go on, but he knew he had to let him tell it in his own time.

'She told me quite definitely she wanted to break off our relationship, that she couldn't even contemplate marriage at the moment. She assured me it was nothing to do with me. She liked me, even more perhaps, but that at the moment any permanent relation-ship was impossible.'

He stopped and turned back towards Rob. The latter could see he was upset, his face pale, his hand shook as he lighted a cigarette. 'What happened to her? What happened to us? Was it my fault? What did I do? I don't know the answers to any of those questions. I only wish I did. Over and over again I've asked myself those questions, and dozens of others. Whatever it was that happened, whether she had met someone else, I don't know. But it was enough to change her into a different person, into someone I didn't know, not the Carol Stanton I had wanted to marry . . . That's all I can say. It isn't much help I know, but I have to admit I'm damned glad to have got it off my chest.'

Rob put his hand on his arm. 'I'm sorry, Frank. I really am. I behaved badly, but I think you can guess how I feel, so please forgive me. I'm as much in the dark as you are, but I'm glad to have met you, glad to have had this talk, at least it's cleared the air between us. If I . . . if anything turns up, I'll let you know. Maybe we shall meet again.'

Frank nodded. Then as Rob went out of the door he said.

'If you . . . should there be . . . oh it's none of my business, but if you find out why the poor kid did it, let me know. I'll never rest really till I find out.'

Rob went out into the bright sunshine of the afternoon; the July heat rose from the tarmac of the road. But it was peaceful, ordinary, so different from the dark corners of his mind. It was becoming more and more a tangled web, each time he looked for answers, all he got was more questions.

10

Tea was a hilarious meal. Nora had four foster children at the moment. Always she had up to half a dozen on the farm. One of them, Sadie, had a birthday, at least they thought it was her birthday. She had been found in the classic situation, on the steps of the convent in Wolverhampton, and after several attempts to find the right place for her, she had gravitated to Nora. She was coloured and a diabetic, which had meant she was difficult to place, but just the kind of child Nora loved to enfold in the warmth of her Mother Earth bosom.

It was the first real birthday party Sadie had ever had. Nora had made and iced the cake, there were six candles and her name in pink icing. Everyone had contributed something in the way of presents, from coloured crayons to a grey kitten, which Nora said was to be her special property, she must be responsible for it, feed it and take care of it. Sadie had instantly assumed a new importance. The sad, listless child who had arrived now started to blossom.

As the tempo of the chatter and laughter increased round him, Rob was reminded vividly, poignantly, of his own childhood. He and Carol had been fostered in the town until they came to Nora. He remembered that some time during that first week, it had been late summer when they arrived, she had taken them across the fields of the neighbouring farm. Harvest was finished, and they crossed the stubble in the evening stillness of late summer; heavy, quiet, intensified by a distant, receding train, a faraway milker calling in his cows. He had felt then the necessity to listen to the quiet; he had been used to buses, trams, kids yelling. The memory of that evening, and all that was to come, now brushed the edges of his memory. As they lingered, the mist had folded the distant fields, owls began to call from invisible trees, and it had been warm comfort to get back to the lamplight and warmth of the kitchen — where they now sat — the door open to the summer heat. He could see the hens outside, scratching in the earth about the yard in the rutted crescents of the footmarks of the dairy cows, Blossom and Damsel. Nora milked them twice a day, often helped with enthusiasm, but not much expertise, by some of the children.

He came back to the present as Jackie slapped him on the back. 'Come on daydreamer, you and I are doing the washing up. I'll wash and you dry because you know where to put the things away, I'm still in the learner stage.'

After tea they played on the grass; rounders, croquet with the old battered set he remembered from his childhood. He and Carol had invented racing croquet played from the saddles of push bikes, which had caused many bruises and cuts, all taken to Nora for healing and sympathy. Jackie was wonderful with the children, in her element, teaching them new games, listening to their stories of animals, of school, of the town and the new things they'd seen in the country.

Rob and Nora sat under one of the apple trees, watching.

'She's a lovely lass,' Nora said slowly, 'wish she'd known our Carol better, might have . . . ' She stopped. 'No, I mustn't . . . ' She rested her hand on Rob's. 'I'm glad you've got someone like her, love. She could be a tower of strength if you need it. Often those little ones, the quiet ones, are the strongest when it comes to trouble.'

He knew she had guessed some of what was going through his mind. He pressed her hand, 'Yes, I wanted to see her against this background. It takes a lot of measuring up to. You take a lot of measuring up to,' he grinned at her, 'she's taken to it like a duck to water.'

'Then bring her back whenever you can,' Nora said softly. It was then, suddenly and for no reason, he remembered the 'Scrappy Journals' he and Carol had kept. Cheap exercise books in which they had recorded anything funny or sad or exciting that happened, illustrated with drawings or photos they had taken, a kind of family saga. Nora had said, encouraging them, 'Much easier than a diary, you don't feel you have to write in it each day, so you're much more likely to.'

'Remember our Journals?' he asked Nora now.

'Yes, I still got the ones you kept as kids. Do you still write yours?'

He shook his head, 'No, I often wish I had; got lazy I suppose, or sick of so much form filling in my job.' He broke off. Nora looked at him puzzled.

'What is it? Something you've remembered?'

He shrugged his shoulders, looking

away. 'Oh nothing.' He had remembered now that Carol had once told him she had kept on with hers, and chided him for being so lazy. Somewhere in the flat would be the copies of the recent ones. And amongst them perhaps some information, some clues. Why hadn't he thought of it before? He tried to remember if he had seen any of them on the bookshelves. He couldn't recall doing so, they might be in the bedroom, her desk, anywhere. He felt a burning impatience now to go back and look. As if she sensed some of this, Nora got up.

'Come and give me a hand, this lot have to go to bed some time and perhaps a little male authority will have an effect, otherwise there's going to be no sleep for any of us.'

Jackie bathed the two younger ones, and then read them all a story when they were safely tucked up in the big room where bunks surrounded the walls. Soon heads were drooping, toys dropped to the floor, and peace reigned. The three grown-ups crept downstairs where Nora made coffee and produced a bottle of wine. 'Just to celebrate our meeting, love,' she smiled over the rim of her glass at Jackie.

With a deep content he hadn't felt since the news of Carol's death, Rob knew she had been received into the family.

They drove back to London the next day after lunch, Jackie protesting it was quite impossible to do up the fastenings of her dungarees. 'A week here, and I would be stones heavier,' she laughed as she kissed Nora goodbye.

'It wouldn't hurt you either, lass. You need a bit of nourishing to bring some roses into those cheeks. Can't abide that smoky, dirty, noisy place.' She turned to Rob, 'See you soon love, and bring Jackie with you. Don't bother to let me know, I'm always here.'

She waved them off down the lane, the children crowded round her, two of them tearful at the fact that Jackie had to go, comforted a little by the huge old- fashioned gobstoppers Nora had handed round to distract them a little from the parting.

As they got back on the Motorway, Rob said, 'That's just typical of Nora, every medicine has to have its spoonful of sugar to help it down. She's just the most wonderful person I ever knew.'

Jackie nodded. 'I can see that. I didn't know such characters really existed outside storybooks, but everything you told me about her, before we met, is true. Incidentally, you haven't had a chance to tell me about Frank Barton. Was he any help?'

Rob hesitated, 'Quite honestly I don't know. There's no doubt he's genuine and he was in love with Carol, and wanted to marry her. But she shied off, wouldn't even discuss it. Then he more or less repeated what you had said about her, about the change that came over her.'

Jackie turned and looked at him, 'So?'

'There's something wrong, I know it.

I've known from the very beginning, you could almost say from the moment I got Nora's telegram; but then I told myself I was being ridiculous. But so many things have happened. To start with perhaps only little things, details — like the car, and the state of the garage, and your remarks. But they all added up, and now I'm absolutely convinced something is seriously wrong, something sinister even.' He hesitated. 'I've longed to say all this to you, but I felt you would think I was being imaginative, hysterical even. You see I haven't got anything tangible to go on.'

She was silent for a moment, then she said, 'As it happens, I agree with you. If you have nothing tangible, I have.'

'What?' He turned towards her, making the car swerve. Her face was pale, she looked strained, almost frightened. He slowed down and pulled over towards the hard shoulder as if he were going to stop. She put her hand over his on the wheel.

'Keep driving. Just look in your mirror. There's a maroon car behind us.'

He did as she suggested. She was right. A maroon Rover, one of the big ones, similar to those many police forces use. It was a few yards behind them.

'I noticed it directly we left London yesterday. It tailed us all the way. At the time I didn't place much significance on it. But I did notice that whenever you accelerated, so did he. When you slowed down, he did. Sometimes he kept a couple of cars between himself and us, sometimes he was right on our tail. It was only a little way before Blisford that he actually dropped away, I didn't notice exactly when. I kept telling myself I was being stupid, imaginative. It could just be coincidence. Although actually he stopped for petrol when we did.'

'Coming up the Motorway, as you

say, it could be acceptable, but if he's still on our tail, then that's a bit too much for coincidence.' He glanced in the mirror again. The maroon car was only a few yards behind them now, the road ahead clear.

'Right,' he said angrily, 'we'll give them a run for their money.' He put his foot down and pulled into the fast lane. Jackie watched the needle, 75, 80, 85, and at last 100. She clung to the seat, 'Watch out for the fuzz, you're not supposed to do more than 70 even on the Motorway.'

'Then maybe that's why that joker has faded out,' Rob said, and they both laughed with relief.

'I know, we'll stop for a coffee. I feel in need of some kind of antidote to that incident.'

The café was fairly crowded. The coffee could have been either tea or soup from the flavour. Rob made a wry face, 'Even on the altiplano I get better stuff than this. A llama wouldn't drink it.' He glanced at his watch. 'Best be getting on if you've got those books to mark up.' His old impatience to see if he could find Carol's journals had returned now.

They walked across the forecourt to the carpark. Suddenly Jackie grabbed his arm, 'Don't look round whatever you do, but the maroon car is parked behind that green lorry.'

'Go back to the car, here's the key,' he said quickly. She put out her hand to take the key ring, 'Please be careful. I just don't like the way things are developing.'

'I'll watch it, don't you worry,' he said softly. He doubled back to the side of the café, and casually lighted a cigarette, looking at the menu, watching the door from the corner of his eye.

One or two people came out, mostly in pairs, then a woman on her own, two children — then a man in a lounge suit. Rob watched him cross the forecourt and go behind the lorry, which was just starting to pull out. The man took a key from his pocket and put it in the door of the car and opened it.

Before he could close it, Rob pounced.

'Right. Who the hell are you and why are you following us?'

Without replying, the man banged the door so that Rob had to let go or his fingers would have been crushed. He slammed in the gears and accelerated, nearly throwing Rob on the ground. Managing to regain his balance, he stood for a moment, staring after the car.

'Well at least I've got your number, and I'll never forget your face, you bastard!' he shouted into the empty air.

11

As Rob slowly surfaced from sleep, he could see the sun was shining behind the curtains. At first he couldn't make out what the noise was that had actually woken him — he had got used to the usual cacophony of sound from the mews below as it too became awake. Milk bottles rattled, someone whistled a tune, stopped abruptly and gave a guffaw of laughter as a voice called out. A cat screeched, a car back fired . . . the trip to Nora had been tiring in some ways. He had been under a strain, and the shock of being followed had all added up to a mental exhaustion so that his sleep had been deep and dreamless. Blisford had been a small oasis of peace in the restless turmoil of his mind which increased as each different detail came to light concerning Carol's death. The Journals had been uppermost in his mind when he returned to the flat, but there was no sign of them, he could only conclude that she, like him, had given up keeping them. Perhaps she just didn't have the time, or she had lost interest . . .

Now he knew what the sound had been which had woken him. The rattle of the letter box. He got out of bed and went into the hall. A letter lay on the mat. He picked it up and turned it over, his hands a little unsteady. He had got to the state now of anticipating more mystery, more frustration.

The letter was addressed to Carol. He turned it over. The name of a bank was printed on the flap. He opened it. It contained the standard statement sent out monthly. He went into the kitchen and lit the gas under the kettle. He saw from the figures on the piece of paper that his sister certainly had no money troubles, in fact he was quite surprised at the amount shown in her current account, and very little on the debit side. They had both always been careful with money, it hadn't come easily.

As his eyes took in the printed columns of figures, although it was such an ordinary piece of paper, it brought poignant memories of his sister. He realised that of course the bank didn't know of her death, or if they had heard, no one had told them officially or the statement would not have been issued. That was a job he would have to do . . . and return the hired car in which he and Jackie had gone to Blisford. After that he was going back to the police station to pick up the Mini, and this time he would insist on either having it returned, or knowing why. He felt in a slightly aggressive mood now; perhaps the reason was the thought of that maroon car.

He made some coffee, toasted some bread — he couldn't be bothered with cooking that morning. He missed Jackie's bright company. She'd be on her way to school now.

He drove through the teeming morning traffic, still not really used to the hassle, the scurrying, tense-faced crowds of people, closely packed vehicles which all reminded him of ants on a giant heap that he had once turned over with his foot in South America. How far away all that seemed now; another world, another life. He supposed one day he'd return.

He deposited the car at the garage from where he had hired it and got a taxi back to the police station. This time a young constable wrote down his name, rang through to a sergeant, making Rob wonder if he was once more going to be fobbed off, but to his surprise the man said at once, 'Through this way please, sir.' He led him out to the car park, where a few days ago he had searched for the Mini without success. Now the cheeky little car with its distinctive flower motif, stood waiting. The policeman handed him the keys. Briefly, Rob wondered if he knew the details, knew where it had been all this time and what had happened to it. Probably not, to him it was just another part of the routine of the day.

'Thanks.' He got in and put the key in the ignition. He knew it must be imagination, but he could almost persuade himself her perfume still lingered. There was nothing else, no gloves, no personal knick knacks, only an impersonal AA handbook.

He glanced at the address on the bank statement and drove off, hoping he would find somewhere to park. He was lucky, there was one space left right outside.

He went to the counter marked 'Enquiries', and rang the bell. When the teller came, Rob pushed the statement across to him.

'I'm Robin Stanton, Miss Stanton's brother. I have to tell you — she died recently. I imagine there will be some formalities to conclude, papers to sign. I am her next of kin and shall be closing the account. Perhaps you'd be kind enough to show me what is necessary.'

The young man gave him a swift glance, but there was no recognition of the situation, no curiosity in his expression.

'I am so sorry, sir, very sorry, about your sister.' He lifted the flap of the counter, 'Perhaps you would be kind enough to come through to the office. There will be quite a lot of paperwork to complete, documents to sign. Do you have some kind of identification?'

Rob had his passport, his temporary driving licence, his own cheque book.

'There will be an affidavit to sign and so on . . . ' It all took longer than he had anticipated, even now it couldn't all be concluded, he would have to sign papers in front of a solicitor. The young man left him for a moment amid a sea of forms and documents. When he returned he had a large sealed envelope in his hands.

'These are your sister's personal documents, Mr Stanton. The manager says it will be in order for you to have them.'

Rob looked at him with surprise. 'Documents? I don't understand.'

'They are listed. Her birth certificate, some building society bonds and so on. Many people these days deposit such things with us. There are so many robberies, muggings, nothing seems really safe unless it is locked away in a strong room,' he gave a faint grin 'even that is vulnerable nowadays.'

Rob took the big envelope. It was quite heavy as though it contained more than documents. Going back to the car, he put it on the passenger seat, and then slid under the steering wheel. He started to put the key in the ignition, then he withdrew his hand, turning again to look at the envelope. He picked it up. It certainly was heavy. Surely a few documents such as the young man had described couldn't possibly weigh that much. He couldn't wait to get back to the flat, his curiosity had to be satisfied now.

Carefully, using the ignition key as a paper knife, he slit open the flap, and carefully pulled out the contents.

The papers were clipped neatly

together — bond certificates, her birth certificate, which Nora had managed to get for her from the Social Service people, some premium bond slips . . . underneath were four of five loose leaf jotters. He hardly had to glance at them to know . . . These were Carol's Scrappy Journals, the ones which had filled his mind while he was at Nora's, but why on earth had she thought them so precious that they had to be put in the bank?

He could hardly contain his excitement, his rising curiosity, the feeling that somehow at last he was going to get somewhere.

Quickly, he fiicked through the pages written in the dear, familiar writing that brought a lump to his throat. The early ones were just the same as those they had kept as children, full of details of thoughts, jokes, comments on people. There were one or two photos stuck in. He studied them carefully. There was no man among them, only girls, probably from the office on outings or holidays. She had made some line drawings too, and there were remarks about the letters she had written to him, and comments on the one or two he had replied to — pitifully few he noticed with a feeling of remorse. There was a drawing of a llama as he had described it to her, looking down its nose like a superior duchess. It brought an involuntary smile to his lips, she had filled in a tiara and long, drop earrings.

Each diary held two or three months, depending on how much she thought writing about that was worthwhile. For, as in the past, they were not written up each day, only when something appealed as worth recording, however trifling it might be.

Then gradually he could see a change.

Extracts became shorter. Hardly any of her feelings or thoughts were committed to paper. References to a riding school started to appear, obviously the one to which Jackie had referred. It was as if she had got bored, or just hadn't the time.

His eyes flew over the pages, seeking a name . . . but all that appeared in any way personal were the initials 'V.P.' He was puzzled. Had she been flying high, had she meant to type 'V.*I*.P'? Then suddenly a name was there, Doctor Julian Hackworth, and the word 'Kent' scribbled in beside it. It couldn't be her own G.P. He would have been in London, unless she had gone in for private medicine for some reason.

He was becoming more puzzled than ever. Far from throwing any light on the subject, it seemed the opposite had occurred. With an involuntary shake of his head he put the journals back in the envelope.

There must be something missing, something that seemed to tug at the fringes of his mind, something vitally significant.

He would go through them again, read every word, every detail, when he got home.

But before that, he had something else to do.

He started the engine and, letting in the clutch, drove off in the direction of Whitehall . . .

12

From the details which Jackie had been able to give him, he knew where the offices in Whitehall were in which Carol had worked at one time, and that the name of her immediate boss had been Jackson. He would have liked to go straight to the top with his enquiries, to the Commander, but he supposed that was asking too much. In any event, often one got more information from underlings, the top brass had learned the great art of 'diplomacy', which he would have described as 'devious avoidance of a direct answer to any question'.

Going up in the lift his mind was revolving around the entries in the journal. Was this going to be the 'V.P.' she had mentioned?

A deep voice called, 'Come!' in answer to his knock. The man was standing looking out of the window as he entered, but he swung round as he heard Rob closing the door behind him.

'Ah, Mr Stanton,' he moved across to the desk and indicated a chair, 'please, do sit down.' As Rob sank into the leather chair, he studied the man who sat opposite him, fingers together, his back to the light, reminding him of the police officer he had seen. Was this perhaps standard practice by the 'establishment?' But there was no mistaking the warmth of his tone as he said, 'I am so very sorry about your sister, Mr Stanton. We were all sorry. I can assure you you have the very deepest sympathy of the whole department who knew her.' He paused a moment, then went on, 'If there is anything I can do, any way in which I can help, please say so.'

For a moment Rob hesitated, then he said abruptly, 'To be honest I am not particularly happy about the circumstances of my sister's death, Mr Jackson.' The sun now filled the office and Rob could see the other man's face quite clearly. He was regarding him keenly. Without speaking he got to his feet, came round the desk and took hold of Rob's arm.

'Look, I think it would be a good idea if we went somewhere private, somewhere where we can talk.' He turned to a girl who sat in one corner of the room, typing from an audio machine, 'If anyone wants me, I shall only be a short time, Miss Vincent.'

She nodded, glancing for a moment at Rob. He couldn't quite fathom the expression on her face — was it pity, curiosity, or something else? Whatever it was, it was fleeting, and gone before he could really pin it down.

Mr Jackson led him along the highly-polished passageways. 'The corridors of power,' Rob thought with a momentary shaft of amusement. They climbed two flights of stairs and entered a huge room with a domed ceiling; a glass chandelier hung in the centre, a long, shining table stretched the whole length of the room, with telephones, blotters, pens and pencils laid out on it in regimented order.

'The Conference Room,' Jackson said, going towards the double windows which led onto a balcony high above the city. The view was quite breathtaking across the buildings away to the shining river with its ever-moving life. Pigeons cooed and fussed, striding up and down, pecking at imaginary morsels of food. As the doors opened, they flew away in a cloud, their wings sounding like clapper boards.

Jackson leant on the parapet, 'I often come up here, it's so peaceful, the traffic, the seething life below only a faint echo, and the river, somehow timeless, with all its past history. It makes one feel small, insignificant in the order of things. As the poet said 'Men may come, and men may go, but I go on forever'.

Rob was becoming a little impatient. He opened his mouth about to speak, when the man said, 'You are not happy about your sister's death. Is there some particular reason?'

'I can't explain it, put it into words. We were very close always. I know, as certain as I stand here, she did not commit suicide.'

'Perhaps it was strange, but we have to remember none of us ever entirely knows another human being. Some things must always remain an enigma. How often do we see pictures of a man convicted of some crime, murder perhaps, and say 'he doesn't look like a murderer,' but there were dark parts of his mind no one knew about. Although I must say your sister always struck me as a fun-loving girl — happy, a sunny nature. Although she did change in some ways it is true . . . '

Rob stiffened. So even this man had noticed. 'Yes,' he said bitterly, 'so everyone I talk to tells me, but what changed her, that's what I want to know, and I intend to find out.' He knew his impatience must show, but he didn't care.

'I can understand your feelings, Mr Stanton.' Jackson held out a packet of cigarettes, 'Smoke?'

Rob shook his head, 'No thanks.'

With maddening deliberation the man lighted his own, blowing out a cloud of smoke, and saying slowly, 'Be careful, very careful, Mr Stanton. You may turn up a stone and uncover too much, things you don't wish to see . . . to know about.'

Rob was alert at once, 'Just what do you mean by that?'

The man looked at him in surprise; whether it was real or simulated he couldn't judge. 'Only that you might not like what you discover, it's as simple as that. If Carol was behaving so oddly, then has it not occurred to you that there was quite obviously something wrong in her private life?'

Once more a feeling of utter helplessness overcame Rob, so that he found it difficult to speak. He was absolutely certain that was not the case, it was not Carol's private life that had driven her to suicide, indeed she had not been driven to such an act he was certain — it was something to do with her job, something that had gone on within the walls of these gloomy buildings.

The man took him down in the lift. 'You might well get lost here, it is like a maze, in fact some of the people even on the same floor as myself are not known to me.'

Rob murmured something in reply, a feeling once more of utter frustration filling him. He shook hands and went out to the car. For a moment he screened his eyes against the glare of the sunshine after the dim closeness of the building.

As he reached the car and opened the door he saw a scrap of paper tucked under the windscreen wiper. That was all he needed! A parking ticket. He glanced at his watch. He'd not been in there more than forty minutes, if that.

He snatched up the paper and was about to crumple it up and throw it in the gutter, when he saw it was not a printed form but a piece torn from a notebook with some handwriting scribbled on it.

He got into the car and straightened the paper out, his brows drawn together in a puzzled frown. The words were printed as if to emphasise their importance. 'MEET ME AT THE BLUE DUCK CAFÉ JUST ROUND THE CORNER.' There was nothing else, no signature, nothing. In a way he was not really surprised, not really puzzled. Instinctively, subconsciously he had known all along that eventually something of this kind must happen. It was inevitable. He glanced round quickly. For a moment he couldn't see anyone who might have written the note. People hurried by, intent on their own affairs. Then in the mirror he caught sight of a girl standing against the railings, staring at him.

He got out of the car, fumbling deliberately as he locked the door, giving her time, if she needed it. Out of the corner of his eye he could see her walking slowly away. He let her gain a little distance, then he started to follow her.

Round the corner was the 'Blue Duck', a swinging sign hung above the door, there was no mistaking the bright blue bird with a red eye. Inside was the inevitable self-service. He went to the counter and bought a coffee. She was sitting alone at a table in the corner, half-hidden by a coat stand. Slowly he went over.

'Mind if I sit here? The place seems rather crowded.'

She nodded without speaking. He sipped his coffee, wondering if he should wait for her to make the first move. He raised his eyes. She was watching him, her gaze steady. Then, hardly above a whisper, she said, 'I think perhaps I can help you, Mr Stanton.'

He leant forward eagerly now, perhaps at last . . . 'How?'

'I'm Jenny Lapford. I used to work

with Carol, before she was moved that is. She was with Environment, but for some months she worked somewhere else, and she did seem to change into quite a different person. She became somehow — well . . . it seems ridiculous to say it, but mysterious, uncommunicative. She used to talk about some 'assignment' she had been given, but she said she couldn't discuss the details. Actually she had told me that on our last date. She never kept the next one, then I heard she had died. I'm so sorry I can't really be more help than that, or tell you much more, but just that it preyed on my mind, I had to tell someone, say how strange I thought it was, so when I heard you'd been to the inquest, somehow I had to see you.'

Rob wasn't going to let this opportunity slip now. 'Look Jenny, please, this is absolutely vital to me, try to remember — anything, anything she said, anything she might have let slip.'

'There was this riding school she kept on about . . . '

'A riding school. Are you sure? You see she did mention that in . . . well in some old diaries. Somewhere there is a clue, I'm certain of it. I've been looking through them, she had deposited them in the bank. It seems odd, that. Did she tell you the name of this place?'

Jenny shook her head, 'No, just somewhere in Kent, not far from Sevenoaks. I wasn't able to ask her any more. You see I would have liked to go too, I love horses, but directly I suggested it, she clammed up.'

'I see. And there isn't any more?'

She shook her head, 'no, I'm sorry. It sounds feeble, but I just had this feeling that something was wrong. You know.'

Rob got to his feet, 'Indeed I do, and thanks for telling me what you have, at least it confirms some . . . well some ideas of my own. I'm very grateful. Look, here's my phone number, if you do think of anything more, please ring me, any time, day or night, it doesn't matter.'

She took the slip of paper and put it in her handbag. 'OK.' She didn't look at him now as she got to her feet, 'I must get back to the office or they'll miss me.'

Rob couldn't wait to tell Jackie of this latest development. He drove to the school, he knew she'd be out at four o'clock, and as he drew up she came out, surrounded as always by a crowd of delighted, shouting, laughing kids. How normal it all seemed after the kind of nightmare world he seemed to have got involved in.

For a moment her smile faded as she saw him, then she waved and ran towards the car. He got out and went round to open the passenger door for her. She threw herself down in the seat. 'God, I'm tired. Must be a hangover from our trip, not used to these long journeys, Motorway lag. But I did enjoy it, specially that gorgeous food, and meeting Nora of course.' She grinned at him now as he got back into the driving seat and started up the engine. Quickly her hand shot out and rested on his arm.

'Put your seat-belt on!'

He glanced at her, surprised at her agitation.

'OK. I usually do wear it anyway — well one has to now or you can get clobbered. It takes a bit of getting used to. I never bothered in South America, there aren't any police or wardens where I work! Silly really, in a major accident one would probably wish one had — or be glad they had — depending on the outcome!' He stopped short. She was shaking, upset, near to tears. Surely it couldn't just be the seat-belt bit ... he had noticed she was very particular to do hers up on their trip to the Midlands but he hadn't realised it was quite so vital to her. He decided to say nothing for the moment.

They drove to the mews in silence. He glanced at her a couple of times and saw her eyes were closed, her lashes wet. She did look tired, drawn. He could imagine kids of the age she had to deal with were probably little hellers, however much one liked them.

He drew up outside the flat. She opened her eyes. 'Sorry. I'm rotten company, but come in for a cup of coffee, I'll try to liven up a bit.'

'Thanks, I'd like that, I'll just put the car away.'

For a moment, in the garage, he stood looking at the Mini, walking round it like a cat on hot bricks. There was absolutely nothing about it to indicate anything had been done to it, that it had been tampered with in any way. It was neat and clean as a new pin. Slowly he closed the door and locked it.

Jackie had made coffee, brought out a tin of biscuits, but she was still quiet, none of the usual babbling chat. He felt it must be something he had said or done, but for the life of him he couldn't imagine what.

At last she got up and went over to the little table where the photograph of the young man stood, the one he had first noticed when he came into her flat the day of the inquest. She picked it up and brought it over, laying it on his knee.

'That was Jeff, Jeff Morris. He was a student at the Agricultural College near my parents' pub in Devon. He used to come over in the evenings and help out in the bar sometimes.' She stopped and flopped down beside him.

For a long time she didn't speak, staring out of the window, until at last he said softly, 'If you want to talk about it, I can listen.'

She turned and looked at him, her cheeks wet with tears, her eyes bright. 'I feel you've got enough on your plate without my adding to it, but, well I suppose the wound, or scar, or whatever you like to call it, is healing over; trouble is, what's underneath perhaps never will. We fell in love the spring before last. Oh it was a magic time. I was home for Easter. We went out in his car — picnics, we even swam in April, the water was freezing. The primroses in the banks were super

160

— violets, bluebells, everything seemed as if it had been made for us to enjoy.' She paused a moment. 'Of course it was just the same old spring that had been happening for thousands of years, but to us it was different, it was our spring. He came up here to see me whenever he could, I went home every opportunity I had. Then it was Christmas. I'd promised to go home of course, but he didn't want me to drive down, the weather can be dodgy. I said I couldn't possibly come on the train, I had all the presents and everything to bring. It was our first real row, well argument anyway. So in the end he said he'd come and fetch me.' She got up and went over to the window, her back to him.

He could sense, feel the emotions that were running through her. He longed to go and put his arms round her. Slowly now she went on. He knew she had to say it, to speak the words.

'It was Christmas Eve. They'd given out snow warnings, ice warnings, told everyone who could to stay at home. I tried to get through to see what the roads were like in Devon, to stop him coming, but the lines were down. How I wished I'd said I'd go by train, it's just that the car seemed so much easier. I sat here and waited and waited. He was meant to arrive about teatime so we could be home in time to go to the midnight service at the village church.'

Her voice broke on a sob, but she went on. 'I was still waiting at midnight. I still couldn't get through on the telephone. Then the police came. When they rang the bell I thought it was him, I ran to open it . . . I suppose I knew directly I saw them. There was a policewoman with the sergeant. They were kind, wonderful, but there's not much you can do. In the end you have to say the words. Jeff had been killed instantly in a pile-up on the Motorway. He'd gone through the windscreen. At the inquest they said if he'd been wearing his seat-belt he probably wouldn't have been killed . . . ' She swung round, 'so you see how I feel about someone . . . ' She stopped, dropping her gaze. He wondered for a moment if she had been going to say 'someone I care for'. He held out his hand instinctively, longing to take her in his arms as a great uprush of tenderness overwhelmed him. It was a shock, the strength of his feeling as he realised how much she had come to mean to him, but the words would not come, this was not the moment to tell her, to say anything, he felt sure of that.

By now, with the release of telling, she seemed to have recovered. She gave a crooked smile, 'So you see I wasn't just being a flapping female. It is important.'

She poured more coffee, and put the photo back on the table. 'I hope you don't mind me unloading my misery, but it does help — as I hope you've found out.'

He nodded, and drew her down beside him on the sofa. 'Look, I do have something to tell, something I think will interest you. It's about the Journals, Scrappy Journals we used to keep as kids. I was certain they must be somewhere, that Carol hadn't given up keeping hers, and I was right. They were in the bank. I went there today. They certainly prove how much she had changed; not only that, there is quite a lot of gen . . . about this riding school in Kent, and a name, Dr Julian Hackworth. Does that mean anything to you? Did she ever mention him? He seems in some way to be connected with this riding school.'

Jackie shook her head, 'No, I don't remember his name, but I do remember she said the riding school was somewhere near Sevenoaks — West something or other. Maybe if we looked in the phonebook, in the yellow pages, we could find it.'

'Of course.' He got up. 'I do feel we may be getting somewhere, she must have been suspicious of someone to put the journals in the bank.' He picked up the telephone directory. 'If I can find it,

will you come with me on Saturday?'
He grinned at her, 'I feel more and
more like Sherlock Holmes and I do
need a Doctor Watson!'

Now at last she was more or less
restored to her normal self and she
managed to grin back, 'Of course, I'd
like that.'

13

There seemed to be dozens of riding stables and livery establishments listed in Kent, but eventually Rob found one which could be the answer, Cherry Orchard Stables near Westford.

They left early on Saturday morning. Rob wound down his window, 'It's lovely to get out of London in the summer heat, and smell honeysuckle and wild roses, it's years since I've been in England at this time of year,' he said slowly, 'I regret now, bitterly regret I didn't get a job here so I could be near Carol, but there was something about South America that got to me, some kind of primitive magic perhaps.'

Jackie was driving so Rob could follow the map. She was keeping her eyes on the road for the lanes were narrow now and she had visions of a tractor shooting out of the gateway although most of the fields now had corn standing high but still green.

'Remember your Wordsworth?' she said slowly — 'Taught by his summer spent, his autumn gone, that life is but a tale of morning grass,' not that I mean your autumn, or summer have gone I hasten to add, but just that we simply don't realise the passing of time until something pulls us up short, then it's too late, like me over Jeff . . . but there isn't really any point in regret, remorse. They're as deadly as jealousy — and from what I know of Carol, she would have wanted you to work where you were happiest.'

They were approaching the house now. It was long and low, the tiled roof green with mosses, lichen — and age. A tranquillity hung over the cherry orchards which surrounded it, some trees still bearing the ripe red fruit, for which the area was famous. They had entered through an iron gate, opened rather unwillingly by a surly-looking man who did not respond to their greeting, a high wall ran away from the gates out of sight, but the drive wound through lush fields with white fences where horses grazed. As they drew up at the white painted front door, it was opened and a miscellany of dogs rushed out at them, barking, wagging their tails, snapping at each other in play. Behind came a young man in riding breeches and a blue polo sweater, a check cap on his head and a riding crop in his hand. For one moment Rob wondered if this could be the mysterious 'V.P.' of Carol's Journal. The man grinned, 'Good morning, and what a smasher. Can I help you? I'm Kevin French.'

Rob got out of the car and went towards him, holding out his hand. Immediately, one of the spaniels and a border collie leapt up at him, licking his fingers.

'Down Vic! Jess! Where are your manners? I'm so sorry, it's just that they either take a liking to you or not, and the former seems to be the case with you.' He grabbed the dogs by their collars.

'Please don't worry, I love dogs and I'm very flattered,' Rob said. 'I'm Robin Stanton, and this is Jackie Fremington.'

'Nice to see you. Come along in, or did you want to go and look at the stables first? I take it you've come to book a ride.'

'Actually I'm afraid not, but there is something I would like to have a chat about if you could spare a couple of minutes. I'm Carol Stanton's brother, you may not remember her, but she used to come here to ride quite often it seems.'

As Rob spoke, Kevin's expression changed, it was as if the sun had gone behind a cloud. Was he wary, suspicious now, or was Rob letting his imagination run away with him? Without reply, the man turned and whistled the dogs to heel, going towards the front door.

'I think you'd better come inside.'

The old farmhouse was just as Rob had imagined, a flagged hall with a vase of flowers on an oak chest, a huge fireplace with smoke-stained hearth, logs ready laid for the winter fires, shining brasses, dark beams and a smell of beeswax and lavender. Kevin led them into the parlour with its low ceiling and wide window seat, with a view of fields and trees, the Weald of Kent spread out, Rob could imagine how Carol had loved it all. In the distance, among the enormous trees, was a big house, a stately home, so it was obvious this was just the home farm for the estate.

'Please sit down.' Kevin indicated the chintz-covered chairs. 'Now how can I help? I'm afraid, although I remember her, I didn't know Carol all that well. She was a nice kid, and a good horsewoman. In fact she could have become quite outstanding if she'd wished . . . at least . . . ' He broke off as if he had been about to say too much.

Rob said quickly, 'At least what? Please be frank with us. You see both

Jackie and I are convinced Carol didn't kill herself.'

Kevin glanced at him quickly when he had finished speaking. 'As a matter of fact it's strange you should say that because when I read about her suicide in the paper, at first I found it difficult to believe, she had been such a joyful kind of person. Then, a little while ago, before she stopped coming, she did seem to change, as if she was preoccupied somehow. But even so, she just wasn't the kind of person to take her own life surely?'

'Was there anyone special here that she rode with or talked to? Did she bring anyone down with her, or come with someone? Particularly was there anyone with the initials 'V.P.' do you know?' Rob was watching the other man's face closely. Did he imagine it again or did Kevin's expression change? But before he really had time to be sure, the man got to his feet.

'I'm sorry, it was very strange but — well — I suppose these things happen and really I can't throw any light on the subject at all. Now, you must excuse me, I am expecting a pupil.'

Rob and Jackie got back into the car. He was bitterly disappointed. For some reason he had had high hopes that this was going at last to produce something really tangible, all he had proved was that it was since she had been coming here she had changed, but not the reason . . .

They had nearly reached the iron gates, which now stood open, when suddenly a car turned in from the lane outside. It came straight at them, travelling at speed. Jackie slammed on the brakes, the car slid sideways in the ditch at the side.

'You bloody maniac!' Rob shouted, but the words died on his lips as the car, without making any attempt to slow up or stop, swept on past them, only inches to spare between the two vehicles.

'My God!' he turned round to watch

it vanish up the drive. 'That's matie in the maroon car, the one who followed us, the chap I saw in the Motorway café . . . so something *is* going on here, just as I thought. We haven't drawn a blank after all.'

Jackie had managed to manoeuvre the car back on to the drive. 'Do you want to go back?'

Rob shook his head slowly, 'Not now, but later — yes — I'll be going back all right.'

They drove back to London with a feeling of shared excitement now, discussing the entries Carol had made in the Journals — and Kevin — who had seemed genuine enough, but was he? And who was this man in the maroon car who kept turning up as if he knew their movements?

When they reached the mews Jackie said, 'Coming up for some coffee?'

He shook his head, 'Thanks all the same, but I'm going to read through those Journals again, see if there is anything I missed, and do some quiet thinking. I'll see you later, and thanks for driving.'

He ran lightly up the steps to the flat, the key ready in his hand, impatient to return to the diaries. He really felt a door was at last slowly starting to open.

As he entered the flat a faint smell of cigarette smoke greeted him. He crossed the hall. The door into the sitting room was open. The sight that met his eyes brought a gasp of horror to his lips. The room was in a complete chaos. Chairs were over-turned, cushions ripped open, drawers upset on the floor, their contents scattered, all the books had been taken from the shelves. Immediately he bent down and searched the volumes on the floor.

It didn't take long to confirm his suspicions. The Journals were gone, every one of them. All his elation dissolved and, like a slap across his face, a terrible thought struck him. There was only one person he had told about the Journals — Jackie. There was only one person who knew he would be away from the flat today — Jackie. It wasn't possible. He felt disloyal even to let the thought enter his mind — and yet there were little details over the past days — things she had told him about Carol which normally a disinterested person would not have noticed. But was his imagination running away with him now? He racked his brain. No one else could possibly have known about the Journals. And to think he had trusted her, taken her into his confidence, cared for her, even fallen in love with her.

There was a pain in his heart that was almost physical. He thought of the times they had shared, of her laugh, her gentleness with the children at Blisford . . . even Nora must have been taken in by her . . .

If she were indeed part of the deception then the whole of his faith in human nature was utterly destroyed. Nothing was left worthwhile — nothing.

He sank heavily onto the torn sofa and dropped his head on his hands in despair.

He had come to the end of his tether . . .

14

How long Rob sat with his head in his hands he had no idea. Thoughts, scenes, emotions chased across his mind like clouds in a storm-tossed sky.

Looking back over the last few weeks of his life he was reminded of the wall chart they had in his office in South America — a chart beloved of the board of directors. It showed a red line climbing to a peak of output, of success; then, for no apparent reason, the line dropped as rapidly as it had ascended, sometimes almost to rock bottom. Thus the line on his personal chart had hit the bottom, the nadir, when he heard of Carol's death. It had stayed at that level until he had met Jackie and got to know her. She had given him renewed strength, faith, a reason to keep on; the very knowledge that someone cared had meant so much.

Now that peak had plummeted again, below rock bottom, if it was possible.

He lifted his head, screwing up his eyes against the light. Long fingers of sunshine shone through the windows, motes of dust danced in the beams. He noticed everything in detail, as if it were very important, as if he had to grasp, and hold on to something tangible in a world that had suddenly become a quicksand. No — that wasn't quite true. He had experienced the quick-sands before; but then there had been a hand held out, warm, soft, strong, yet gentle.

With an exclamation wrung from the depths of his being, he got to his feet, pulled the last cigarette from the packet and lit it, throwing the empty carton on the floor.

Now that his first feeling of shock had passed, he felt a growing anger. It started somewhere deep inside. He felt it swelling, expanding like a nuclear explosion, filling his whole frame with a dark, mindless fury. For a moment he felt like simply walking out of the flat, locking the door and leaving the mess for someone else to clear up — a faceless someone — slowly that someone took shape and became Jackie.

She could clear it up. She who could be the cause of it. He inhaled deeply. Slowly the nicotine brought some relief from the tension. Even that brought some satisfaction — the thought of the harm it was probably doing his lungs. He had meant to give up smoking, had even managed to cut down, now he felt a futile, immature delight in the thought of how sorry people would be if he became seriously ill — especially her . . .

As he relaxed a little, he started to pick up some of the rubbish, to attempt to tidy the chaotic mess. He found a cardboard carton in the kitchen that had held groceries, and rammed the papers and torn books into it. Even that gesture brought a little gratification.

Now he searched his mind for someone else who could have done this. But all the time his thoughts returned to Jackie, to the conviction that no one else could have added up all the information and known just where and when to look for the diaries.

Oh God! If only he knew if she were implicated. His heart told him it couldn't be true. His head told him it was possible, that anything in the world of intrigue, in which he seemed to have become involved, in which now he knew Carol must have been involved, anything was possible, anyone could be called Judas.

As he calmed a little, he became more certain of one thing. He was going to get to the bottom of this evil. He was going to stop pussy-footing around, being polite, not hurting people's feelings, not appearing to be nosy or over-curious. From now on he was going out for concrete facts no matter how he had to tackle the people who seemed involved, and even those who did not appear to be, he told himself grimly. Ruthlessness was no part of his make up, something utterly alien to him, but he would cultivate it from now on.

He stopped picking up the pieces. Feathers from one of the cushions still floated in the air. He got a plastic bin liner from the kitchen to put them in and, while he was there, put coffee on to percolate. He'd have to go out and get some cigarettes, there were none left. He was appalled at the number he had smoked, surprised it was still only afternoon. So much had gone through his mind in such a short time he felt hours, not minutes, must have passed.

Once more he got out the notebook in which he had first written down his plans for action. He put a line through them, then wrote — 'Priority One — Kevin French and the Riding School'.

He tapped his teeth with his pencil as he thought about it . . . He'd go back there and confront Kevin, somehow everything seemed to be tied up, to come back, to that place. He thought of his recent visit with Jackie, the maroon car . . . Jackie — what was he going to do about her? Should he tell her of his thoughts, his plans? He still felt uncertain, bewildered, as he thought of her. He just couldn't be sure that she was not on 'their' side, involved with his 'enemy' — whoever that might be. Even that he did not know. It was like living in a fog, an impenetrable, shifting mist which he had thought now and then had lifted, but yet seemed thicker than ever.

Was he losing his touch over assessing people? He had grown to love Jackie, felt about her as he had never felt over anyone before, and he had begun to think perhaps she felt the same way about him.

He thought of her at Nora's; with the children; at the school where she worked, the way she behaved with them and the way they responded — the way she had been with him.

She had seemed so genuine, he had been so sure, so secure. He had never felt the same confidence with anyone before — except perhaps Nora — but that had been a different emotion, a child for a mother figure. Jackie had been a beloved companion, to begin with, and then something more, something so much more. Now this doubt had crept in, the feeling that he simply could not trust her.

He got up and went over to the window. For a long time he stood looking across the mews at the windows of her flat. He glanced at his watch. It was long after the time she should be home, but the windows were dark. She must still be out. In a way he was thankful. Had she been there he might have been tempted to go across, to face her with his doubts and ask for reassurance. That was something he must resist at all costs until he was sure. He owed Carol a debt and, before anything else, that had to be paid.

Wearily he went into the kitchen and

cooked himself some eggs and bacon. But when it was ready he pushed it round on his plate. He had no stomach for it. He drank two cups of coffee. There was a bottle of whisky in the cupboard, half full. He poured some into a glass and drank it neat in a couple of swallows. It burnt his throat as it went down, and for some reason the feel of it brought a little sanity back to him. Tomorrow he'd take positive action. 'After all, tomorrow is another day' — the closing words from *Gone With The Wind*; that too, had been a tale of love, and hate, treachery and betrayal.

Much to his surprise, he slept well, and late. The sun was high above the roofs of the mews. Quickly he showered and dressed, gulped down a cup of black coffee, then remembered he had no cigarettes. He'd have to get some before he could face the problems of the day. He opened the door and ran down the steps into the street. He opened up the garage and drove the car out. As he did he heard footsteps running lightly towards him. He knew before he turned that it would be Jackie. His heart quickened its beat. She pulled open the passenger door and jumped into the seat like a small girl, confident as a child that she would be welcome.

She grinned up at him, 'I was just coming to see you. I was a bit late in last night, PTA meeting you know, and I didn't see any light in the flat so I thought perhaps you'd had an early night. Where are you off to?'

He said quickly, without looking at her, 'I thought I'd take a run up to see Nora.' He fiddled with the ignition key, switching off the engine, turning it on again, running his fingers round the edge of the steering wheel. Her nearness, the sweet perfume that always hung about her, brought a wave of longing, of deep emotion, which he could not resist. He longed to take her in his arms, to say, 'Darling Jackie, I love you, I want to marry you. Tell me you are on my side, tell me you're not my enemy.' The emotion was so strong he was surprised she didn't sense it and respond. Still he didn't look at her.

He knew she must be thinking it was so unlike him — the hurried answer, the averted gaze. She said uncertainly, 'Oh . . . ' then she put her fingers on the door handle, gripping it as if she needed its support, her knuckles white. He had never appeared like this before. Usually he was one of the warmest people she had ever known. 'I . . . ' she hesitated. It was Saturday, he knew she didn't have to go into school. There was no reason not to ask her to join him.

She waited, still-half expectant. 'Has something . . . '

He guessed she was going to ask him if something had happened, but couldn't bring herself to probe. If anything had, she would be sure he would tell her.

Now she pushed the door open, bending forward slightly as she did so, her hair falling over her face. 'Well, I'll see you when you get back.' She grinned. It was a tight smile and now he turned and looked at her. His eyes were pleading. She looked back. There was nothing she could say. How could she know what he was pleading for?

'Yes,' he said, forcing a lightness he did not feel into his voice, 'Yes, OK. I'll see you later.'

He started the engine, let in the clutch, made a hash of the gears, and drove off in a series of kangaroo hops. He could see her in the mirror. She stood forlorn, desolate, and he felt for a moment as if he had physically assaulted her in some way.

It was with the greatest difficulty he stopped himself from turning the car round and going back to take her in his arms.

15

For some time he drove through the morning traffic with no purpose. Several times irate and vociferous taxi drivers blew their horns, shook their fists, and shouted at him. He was still unused to the frenetic London traffic and, even more, to the one-way systems which seemed like some kind of giant maze. Eventually he found himself approaching the outskirts of London towards the Motorway that led to the Midlands.

He would do as he had told Jackie on the spur of the moment; he would go and see Nora. For one thing the drive would give him time away from the flat, away from Jackie, to sort things out in his mind. He needed time to think — most of all he needed Nora's calm, commonsense. Perhaps she held the answer to some of the questions.

He began to feel a little better as soon as he reached the lane that led to the house. He parked the car and jumped out. As usual the kitchen door stood open. A miscellany of dogs, cats, chickens and geese greeted him as he crossed the yard and went in. Nora was at the sink; she turned, and an expression of joy and tenderness suffused her face as she held out her arms, uttering his name. He went to her like a small child seeking comfort once more as she held him to her ample breast. Then she said, 'There, I've put soap all over your nice sports jacket.' She looked up at him, her eyes gentle, but enquiring like a robin.

He held her for a moment, 'Why is it you always smell so nice — an indescribable kind of smell — soap, polish, lavender, country smells . . . '

'And chips with everything!' she grinned, gently releasing herself. She knew already from the expression in the beloved eyes that something was wrong, very wrong but, as always, she would not probe, she would wait. Eventually it would come out.

'I suppose you've had no breakfast?' Her back was turned now as she filled the kettle and put it on the stove. A lamb lay in a basket beside the solid fuel cooker, its eyes closed, the small black nose resting on the edge of a blanket.

'Who's the newcomer?' he avoided answering her question.

'From the farm. The ewe had triplets. I'm bottle feeding it,' she grinned, 'worse than having a baby, every two hours, day and night, poor little mite.'

As if it knew it was being talked about, the lamb opened its eyes and gave a faint bleat. Nora went over and picked it up, holding it close for a moment. The lamb snuggled against her as she stood looking down at it. Then she put it back in its box and covered it up with the blanket once more. It gave a little sigh and settled down quietly. It was the kind of soothing effect, the reassurance Nora had on man and beast alike, Rob thought.

He sat down at the scrubbed table while she poured tea from the big enamel teapot he remembered as a child. Often, when they had gone to help with the hay or corn harvest at the neighbouring farm, it was Nora who had brought tea for all the workers, great slabs of homemade fruit cake, homemade bread still warm from the oven, dishes of cream and homemade jam, and the brown enamel teapot.

Suddenly he felt hungry for the first time in days. She put the thick frying pan on the stove; into it went rashers of bacon, tomatoes, mushrooms and a couple of sausages. The smell was tantalising. She sat down with her own cup of tea, looking at him thoughtfully. For a moment he dropped his gaze, but hers was compelling and he had to look up. She said, 'You haven't given up have you love?' with a slight smile curving her lips.

He shook his head. There was no

need for explanation. 'I'll never give up! Never!' he said vehemently. Now he smiled, but it was a travesty. She noticed the strained, bleached look he had, like someone recovering from an accident or a serious illness, as if his skin was stretched too tightly across the bones of his face.

'Do you want to talk?' She got up now and put the food from the pan on a plate, placing it in the keep hot oven of the stove while she broke golden-yolked eggs into the fat.

He sighed. 'I don't seem to get any further, Nora. Each time some little bit of information does look as if it is leading somewhere, then a blank wall looms up, just like when you are lost in a fog, and you go round and round on the self-same spot, because the way she died — Carol would never have done that, never. Nothing could possibly be more out of character.'

She finished cooking the meal and put it in front of him. She knew that he would never give up, he had never been a quitter, even when he was a small boy. She remembered during carpentry classes at school, he had been making a surprise for her, a nesting box to fix near the kitchen window for the tits. Three times he had had to remake it because something had gone wrong. She had found him in the barn, his tongue stuck out with concentration, his small frame quite rigid with determination to finish it and to make it properly. He had, and it still stood outside on the sill. No, Rob would never give up — that was partly what worried her now as he seemed to have changed so much, even from the last time she had seen him. There was a set look about his lips, a look in his eyes she had never seen before. She was deeply concerned for him.

As he ate she sipped her tea. At last he put down his knife and fork, the plate cleared. He mopped up the juice with a piece of bread. Some of the strained look had gone as he grinned at her.

'That was the best meal I've had since I came back to London.' He blew her a kiss with his fingers. She got up and re-filled his cup.

'Can you tell me what's wrong, love?'

He lighted a cigarette before he answered; then he said, 'If you had a friend, a very special, dear friend, and you found out she had deceived you — at least you were pretty sure on all the evidence, that she had, what would you do? How would you deal with the situation?'

Now it was her turn to pause before she replied. Then she said slowly, looking directly into his eyes. 'If she were my friend, then I would refuse to believe it, particularly if it were based on circumstantial evidence without proof of any kind.'

His smile was wry as he said, 'Sometimes it's not as simple as that.'

She got to her feet, 'Life is never simple, human beings are not simple, even animals sometimes are complex. Perhaps that's partly what keeps us going, the joy of finding out what does make people tick, and finding out we can be wrong — or right — about them.'

He glanced at his watch. 'I'll have to go. There are things I want to do.'

Even as he uttered the words he wasn't sure what the things were, but now he felt refreshed in mind as well as body to some extent. He got to his feet. 'It isn't really a very nice thing to do to anyone — drive up here, let you cook me a meal, gobble it down and then say 'thanks', and dash off!'

Once more he put his arms round her and for a moment rested his head on her shoulders. 'But you are like an oasis in a desert, a kind of rehabilitating comfort station!'

She threw back her head and laughed. He could feel it rumbling up inside her. 'You make me sound like some kind of service station for camels!' Now he too laughed, and she was glad to see the tension eased. 'Anyway, that's what I'm for, rest and refreshment, this is your home, if you couldn't use it that way it would cease to be a home.'

She followed him to the door, 'Just as long as you keep coming back, that's all I mind.' She was about to say 'and not back to that horrible heathen South America,' but she bit back the words. As always, people were left to make their own decisions where Nora was concerned. 'How's that nice Jackie, by the way? You should have brought her with you.'

He turned at the door. Once more she saw the clouds return to his face. She had known at once, when he had asked the question, that Jackie was the 'friend' to whom he had referred. She knew too that he was fully aware of this fact. She realised something of the cause of his mood, of the change — because he had doubts about Jackie. Something had happened. She didn't know what, but he would tell her in his own good time. She said, 'You know, the minute I met that girl I liked her, knew she was entirely trustworthy and sincere. Straight as a die. I'd risk my life on that. Kids know at once, and look at the way they reacted. You can't fool a child where honesty and sincerity are concerned.'

Now he looked her full in the face.

'But you thought that about Carol — yet she concealed more of her private life than anyone thought possible.'

It was as though he had driven a dagger into her heart. She was right, all this had changed him, once he could never have said such a thing to her.

16

As he drove away from Blisford, he thought about his last remark. He hadn't meant to hurt her, but he knew he had. The words had come out almost as an accusation, on the spur of the moment, simply because his own mind was in a turmoil. He hoped she would understand. It was more than likely that she would, for although she hadn't answered him directly she had managed to smile and squeeze his hand as he left. He wondered how much that had cost her . . .

And now suddenly he was brought back to more mundane things. The Mini had developed an ominous rattle as if part of the engine was about to fall off. Quickly he pulled into the side of the road, thankful he hadn't yet reached the Motorway.

'Damn and blast!' he said aloud as he

got out of the car. He didn't want to hang about, any small delay seemed magnified at the moment, but it was still a long way to London, and he couldn't risk the Motorway in an unroadworthy car. He bent down and looked underneath. The cause of the trouble was immediately obvious. The exhaust manifold had come loose and was rattling against the chassis. Maybe Frank could patch it up with what they called 'gun gum' just until he could have it serviced.

He turned the car round and drove back to the garage.

Frank was delighted to see him; he came towards Rob, wiping his hands on an oily rag.

'Hi there! Nice to see you. Been up to Nora's?'

Rob nodded, 'Yep. I've got a problem. The exhaust seems to have come loose, I was just wondering if you could do a temporary job so I can get back to the Smoke.'

'Let's have a look. Run her into the

199

shed, there's an inspection pit there. I'll give it the onceover.'

He reappeared from the pit after a few seconds.

'That's damned odd. There's a bracket been put on the wrong way round by some cowboy, and of course it's worked loose, that's what's rattling.'

'Why is it odd? That kind of thing seems to happen all the time with modern cars.'

'Yeah, I know that, but I put on a new exhaust for Carol last time she was up here,' he looked away for a moment, then he said, 'not long before she died. It can't have needed anything doing to it, I do a good job when I do it, not that kind of shoddy mock-up.'

Rob looked at him sharply. 'Have another look underneath would you?'

Frank crawled back under the car, then he ran his hand along the rear bumper. He gave an exclamation and, withdrawing his hand, held up a small metal object. Rob took it from him.

'What on earth is that? Nothing to do with the exhaust system surely?'

Frank was no longer grinning. 'It's a bug.'

The two men looked at each other. Mutual understanding flashed between them. Frank had never really believed Carol committed suicide either. Now he pointed to the object.

'You fix this on the car you want to follow, out of sight of course, it transmits a bleep which operates over quite a considerable distance . . . this is one of the latest type . . . someone with a receiver — either in their hand or in another car — can follow.'

Rob looked down at the piece of metal lying in his palm. It looked so innocent, so ordinary. The very sight of it filled him with revulsion, the idea it represented, the fact that someone had been following Carol, that this piece of metal might have even led to her death. He was about to fling it on the ground, but he changed his mind and slipped it into his pocket.

Frank watched him, his eyes questioning . . . 'What the hell . . . ?'

'I'll let them catch up with me, whoever they are, then I'll KNOW who killed Carol, won't I?'

Rob felt a certain reluctance at leaving Frank. He liked the chap, he was refreshingly sincere and honest, unlike so many people he seemed to have come up against since Carol's death — and that now included Jackie. The agony of his feelings about her was like an open wound, he tried to push it from his mind, but all the time it returned to taunt him. If only there was some way he could prove her innocence. Odd that — it reminded him of British justice which said everyone was innocent until proved guilty. Maybe he was being over-sensitive about her, and yet who else could have known about the diaries he had got from the bank? Who else had known he would be absent at that particular time? He tried to push those thoughts into the back of his mind as he drove down the

Motorway back to Kent — Kent, and not London, because he had decided he was going directly to the riding stables. He was convinced some of the clues he was looking for were hidden there, that perhaps even Kevin French held the key. So what was his approach going to be? What was he going to say to him?

First of all, as he had already decided on the concrete, absolute approach, he was going to tell him that he knew now that Carol did not commit suicide. He was also going to tell him that he knew she had not come to the riding school merely for lessons, that he had proof it was much more than that. It all sounded fine as he rehearsed it from the safety of the car — he was going to have to take his cue from then on via French's reaction.

He drew into a café for coffee, he needed the stimulation it would bring. He smoked a cigarette, his mind still going over his imagined conversation, then, lighting another from the butt of the first, he got back in the car. He drove quickly now and soon reached the entrance to the riding school. He had decided not to approach the house this time, but to go direct to the stables at the side where the small office for arranging the hiring of horses and taking lessons was situated next to the tack room, part of the old buildings. He was prepared now to say his piece.

The entry to the stables was under an archway with a small cupola on the top where a clock now struck the hour in mellow tones. The loose boxes took up three sides of the yard, there were blue painted tubs full of brightly coloured geraniums, doves cooed in a huge dovecot built into the walls, and the horses stood looking over the half doors, curious spectators of any activity in the yard. The whole atmosphere was so peaceful, so ordinary, it was difficult to keep his mind on his resolve. It seemed impossible any kind of violence, intrigue, could have taken place in this atmosphere of calm peace.

The office door opened and a man

came out. Rob opened his mouth to speak, but the man who approached him was not Kevin French. Whoever this was, he must be an employee of Kevin's and he didn't particularly want a report taken back that he had been nosing around the premises, that would put Kevin on his guard. He was anxious to take him by surprise.

'Hi,' he lifted his hand in casual greeting, 'I wondered if I could hire a horse for a ride. I am fairly experienced, shan't need a groom or anyone with me.'

The man looked at him curiously for a moment. 'We like people to have the proper kit, either breeches or jodphurs usually, sir, and boots of some kind, certainly a hard hat. Have you brought something with you?'

Rob shook his head. What a fool he'd been, he should have thought of that. He grinned disarmingly. 'No, as a matter of fact I had a night out last night, stayed with friends, you know how it is. Felt I needed a ride this morning to clear the cobwebs, and I didn't particularly want to have to drive all the way back into town to get my gear. I have ridden in trousers and shoes before — the only thing is, perhaps you could lend me a hat of some kind.'

The man nodded. 'OK. Of course we can't really accept responsibility for accidents if you're not properly equipped, you understand that?'

'Yes, of course.' Rob followed the man into the office where he took a velvet riding hat down from a peg.

'Actually it's mine, but it's a pretty standard size.'

'That's very nice of you, thanks.' Rob put it on, it fitted perfectly. The man handed him a crop.

'You may need this if you're going to try any of the jumps in the park, although most of the horses are pretty well trained, hands and knees should be enough.' He went out into the yard again and led Rob to one of the loose boxes. 'This is Carver Doone, he's done quite a bit of eventing, but he's an honest kind of animal, totally reliable and really good jumper.'

He put the bridle on the horse and led it out into the yard, giving Rob the saddle. He slipped it over and pulled up the girth. The horse was a chestnut with a white blaze. It tossed its head, playing with the bit, anxious now to be off. The man gave Rob a leg up, he gathered the reins and touching his hat with the crop, grinned down at the man, 'Thanks. I'll probably be about an hour. OK?' The man nodded, 'Yes, we're fairly quiet this time of day. You'll find the road that leads to the park on the left there.'

Rob found it pleasant to be back in the saddle, particularly with a well-bred horse, which this obviously was. In South America most of the animals were either broken winded, or mules. This one responded at once to the lightest touch of his heels, and had an easy stride, giving him a comfortable ride. He started to enjoy himself. He cantered, then galloped for a short time over the grassy field which led into the park, a magnificent place of ancient trees, a small stream and winding paths among the shrubs. He had ridden down towards the gate, and back to the farmhouse, looking for the maroon car, but there was nothing but a Land Rover standing next to his own car in the drive.

There were one or two jumps set up in the field, he put the horse to them and he flew over with consummate ease, then once more he set off for the park riding now across to the furthest part which he had not reached before. Suddenly he came to a small driveway with a gate; on it was a notice 'Private. Keep Out'. Somehow the curtness of the words aggravated him, apart from the fact that his curiosity and suspicion were immediately aroused. Riding up to the gate, he bent down. It wasn't padlocked and he managed to open it without dismounting.

Gradually the lane widened and turning a corner he suddenly saw a mansion, a magnificent house, probably Elizabethan he guessed, a type of fortified manor. It was in good repair, the stonework restored, the windows bright in the sunlight. A brick wall ran round it and he guessed there must be a main entrance on the other side. The house where he and Jackie had met Kevin French must be the home farm with the stables attached.

As he reined in his horse and stood looking at the house an odd feeling started to creep over him. It was so silent, so still, as if it had been caught in some kind of timelessness. No birds sang, no dog barked, there were none of the usual country sounds of grass being mown, voices. It was eerie, like the castle in *The Sleeping Beauty*, as if it waited, crouching, for something or someone to rouse it into life.

As he drew closer, he saw that many of the upstairs windows were shuttered, the garden overgrown. It was almost as if it had some secret it was reluctant to divulge.

He rode round the wall. When he reached what he assumed was the front of the house, the wall ran away, probably down the main drive, but it was too high for him to see over the top. He turned the horse. Nowhere had he passed any gate or entrance in the wall itself. He retraced his steps and then went beyond the place where he had first sighted the house. A small path, hardly wide enough to ride along, led away from the wider drive. Here at last was a gate in the wall, lower than the rest of it, only a few feet high, and some of the bricks from the top had fallen to the ground where the ivy had overgrown. He could easily see over the top now, but from here the house was hidden by trees and shrubs. The menace of the atmosphere, the sinister air about the place, had affected him more than he realised. He had to know what went on in that house, he was absolutely convinced now that it was here, not at the stables, that the reason for Carol's visits were to be found.

His next action was completely impulsive.

Without a second's hesitation, he wheeled the horse round so he could give him a short run, praying his training would stand by him as he touched him lightly on the flanks with the crop. He felt the animal tremble and gather itself together; with a snort it soared into the air. Rob lost one of his stirrups, he clung with his knees, grabbing at the thick mane, closing his eyes, the reins loose in his hands now as he felt the animal strain beneath him . . . the horse landed heavily as Rob opened his eyes. In a brief second he saw a man who had obviously been sitting at a table reading. The book lay on the grass where it had fallen. Now the horse reared and caught the table with its front hoofs. Once again he grabbed frantically at its mane as he started to slide backwards . . .

He heard the man shout something — something totally incomprehensible — as he slid away into darkness . . .

17

Rob could have blacked out only for a matter of seconds, but he felt as if a hundred hammers were beating inside his head as once more he opened his eyes.

For a moment he lay where he was on the grass, feeling each limb gingerly to make sure nothing was broken. As he looked up, he saw a man was standing over him . . . It was Kevin French. He struggled to his feet, glad he had borrowed a hard hat for it was badly crushed and he was thankful the dent was in the hat and not his skull. He glanced round for the man who had been reading at the table and who had given a shout as he appeared. There was no sign of him.

French stood with his hands on his hips.

'What the hell is going on?' His voice

was edgy, his gaze suspicious. Without replying, Rob turned to look at the horse, concerned it might have injured itself on the sharp metal table. But it was standing nearby, totally unconcerned as it cropped the grass. The saddle had slipped to one side, and the reins were broken; but apart from that, all seemed well. He went over and patted it on the rump, it turned and whickered at him. Although he was genuinely concerned for the animal, his head was still like cottonwool from the bump he had had, and he decided to play the innocent until his senses returned.

French was tapping his riding boots impatiently with his crop as he said, 'Could you tell me exactly what you were doing — are doing? Don't you know this is private property, not part of the riding school?'

Rob shook his head, hoping very much his expression appeared as inscrutable as he intended it to. 'I'm sorry. I didn't realise . . . '

'I should have thought the wall made it obvious enough, even if you can't read the signs,' French said with heavy sarcasm.

Rob realised the act he was putting on was pretty unconvincing. But he said, 'I really am sorry. It was one of those impulse things, you know. You're out on a beautiful horse — which this one certainly is — ' he turned and stroked the animal once more, 'and I tried it over some of the jumps in the park. It flew over them, jumped like a cat. I simply couldn't resist the temptation to try it against something with more of a challenge. I'm sure I don't have to tell a horseman like yourself the feeling that comes over one sometimes — although I would hardly compare my ability with yours . . . '

Slightly mollified, French nodded, 'Well I do know what you mean, but it really is private here, we can't have every Tom, Dick and Harry careering about all over the place, as I'm sure you'll appreciate — and for another thing — if an amateur had attempted that, there would have been a real danger and damage. I think you were a bit lucky if I may say so.'

Some of the fog inside Rob's head was lifting. 'I hope I didn't give that other chap — the one who was sitting at the table — too much of a fright. I simply didn't see him until it was too late.'

French shrugged his shoulders, spreading out his hands, 'I think you did give my brother a bit of a shock. He's been ill, and his nerves are still a bit jangly. We have to be careful. That's why he chose this part of the garden to sit and read.'

He had moved towards the horse now and was holding it by the reins, pulling on the stirrup leather, straightening the saddle and tightening the girth.

'Want a leg up? You know what they say, if you have a fall, you must get up again right away. I'll open the gate, and this time you can go through in the orthodox manner to finish your ride. I'd be glad if you'd take Carver Doone back to the stable, I see he's got a small gash on his fetlock. Nothing much, but it needs washing out.'

Rob re-mounted, gathering the reins and tying the broken end. 'Thanks. And really, I am sorry. I'll pay for any damage of course, and if the horse should need the vet . . . '

French shook his head, 'I don't think that will be necessary.' With a wave of his hand he shut the gate behind Rob, and went back into the garden.

Rob still felt a bit shaky. It was a long time since he had taken a fall like that. 'Must be getting old,' he grinned to himself, thankful that his rash act hadn't led to anything more serious.

He delivered the horse back to the groom, pointing out the gash on its leg, saying he had caught it on one of the jumps in the park. He gave the man a ten-pound note, 'Sorry about the hat, took a bit of a tumble. Please buy yourself another one.'

Going back to the car, he felt he needed a stiff drink and decided to call at the village pub which was only a short distance from the riding school. He had passed it on his way in. He went into the bar and ordered a double scotch. It was still well before lunch-time, and there was only one other man in the bar, obviously a regular ensconced in his own particular corner, reading the paper. He didn't even look up when Rob entered.

He was glad of the solitude himself. He didn't particularly want to have to indulge in small talk, his mind was too full of questions, of odd bits of information, none of which seemed to connect, and yet he was more con-vinced than ever that they did, that somewhere the key was hidden, all the time just eluding his grasp. Why had Kevin let him off so easily? It was blatantly obvious he had been snooping around and that the excuses he had given were weak in the extreme. And who was the mysterious stranger who had been sitting reading, who had let out an involuntary exclamation in a language which he was pretty certain was Russian — and certainly Kevin French wasn't Russian, so how did he come to have a brother who was?

He could kick himself for having fallen like he did because it meant he was too shaky to think properly, to observe the finer points, to realise what was happening. Now it meant he would have to go back to the riding school again. And there was no doubt Kevin French would become suspicious, if he wasn't already, and if he wasn't — then he was more of a fool than Rob thought.

He got to his feet. He could do with another drink, but before he had time to reach the bar to order, the man was greeting someone who had just come in.

'Hallo, Dr Hackworth. Nice evening. Going to have the usual?'

'Thanks Fred. Make it a double, will you?'

Hackworth . . .

Rob knew at once where he had seen that name. In Carol's diaries. His senses were alert now as he turned slowly to look at the man who had spoken. It was the doctor he had seen in court, the doctor who had given evidence at the inquest on Carol . . . So the 'name' in the diary was now standing before him in the flesh.

Leaving his glass on the table, he decided against another drink. He didn't know whether the doctor had come just for one, or if he was in for a session, but Rob intended above all now to keep his mind clear, and it would be easier to be outside and catch him than to follow him from the bar.

He crossed the carpark and got into the Mini, winding down the window so he could see the pub door without moving.

The minutes ticked by. Suppose the doctor made a habit of spending a couple of hours in the bar, had a game of darts, or was meeting someone? He shifted uncomfortably. The seat was not really meant for a six footer, and he was beginning to stiffen up from his fall. He needed a good hot bath . . . At that moment the door opened and the doctor came out. He went across to the only other car on the park, opened the passenger door and put his bag on the seat, then he went round and got into the driving seat.

Rob jumped out of the Mini and ran across, wrenching open the driver's door. The doctor had the key in the ignition. He dropped his hand, his face a mask of surprise, and anger. 'What the hell . . . ?'

Rob held out his hand in an ironic gesture of greeting. 'I'm Stanton, Dr Hackworth. Rob Stanton, Carol Stanton's brother.' Suddenly the man turned ashen grey. He made a small helpless gesture with his hand as if to ward Rob off. He looked like a deflated balloon.

'I see you remember her then, the girl who was murdered,' Rob said. Hackworth could see he had no chance to drive off. Rob was grasping the door firmly, one foot rested on the car.

'Really Mr . . . er . . . Stanton, I think . . . '

By now Rob had grasped his arm, half-pulling him from the car, 'This will only take a few minutes, doctor.' They stood facing each other. 'Why did you lie at the inquest, Dr Hackworth? Why did you imply my sister had committed suicide, perjure yourself?'

The doctor looked so ridiculous, if Rob hadn't been so serious, he would have laughed. The man's mouth hung open like a fish gasping for air, the slight breeze had blown the thin strands of hair he had coaxed across the bald patch so they stood up as if in terror. He was obviously doing his best to keep cool as he said quietly, 'Your sister DID commit suicide, Mr Stanton. There was no question of . . . '

Something inside Rob seemed to snap at the cool effrontery of the man, at the feeling that once more he was being fobbed off, treated like a witless child. He grabbed the lapel of the man's jacket.

'You lied then, and you are lying now. You know it. Everything you said at that inquest was a lie. Now I want to know who put you up to it, and I intend to find out, whatever lengths I may have to go to!'

The doctor struggled to free himself from Rob's grasp. His voice had risen now.

'You're mad! I'll call the police. Take your hands off me . . . ' Suddenly, in complete contrast to his anger, Rob felt ice-cold as he said, 'Go on then, call the police. It might be the best thing because I'm going to blow this thing apart. I'm going to bring the true facts about my sister's death right into the open, Doctor. And you can tell whoever's controlling you that I say so — that is if I don't see him first.'

He now released his hold on the doctor so suddenly that the man staggered against the door of the car. Rob stood with his arms folded, watching him. He knew he would get no further with the man at the moment, but he could wait. It was one more piece in the jigsaw, one more nail in the coffin of the person responsible for this whole deception.

Shakily, the doctor got into his car, muttering to himself. Rob turned on his heel as he drove away.

18

Rob drove slowly home, reaching the suburbs just as the mad evening rush had started. The hordes of cars, buses, vans, taxis, reminded him of lemmings rushing to their mindless doom. Where were they all going? Where had they all come from? And what did they do with those extra few seconds they pared off their frantic journey, when they reached the other end?

He felt exhausted with the events of the day, and now the stiffness, which had threatened earlier, had taken possession of his body. He longed for the benison of a hot bath, and when he'd put the Mini in the garage at last, he went slowly up to the flat, his mind still full of the details of the bug, the Russian, and the doctor ... It was beginning to take on the format of a spy story with all the important bits kept from the reader until the end — he was the reader and he wasn't sure the pieces of the jigsaw were ever going to fit into place. There just wasn't any sense, any reason behind it all.

He had scarcely eased off his shoes and tie, preparatory to running a bath, when he heard footsteps along the hall outside. Someone was in a tearing hurry. There was a pounding on the door. He got up and flung it open. Jackie fell into his arms, breathless, sobbing, one shoe missing. He could feel the fluttering of her heart against his chest, like a caged bird. He smelt the flowerlike perfume of her hair, sensed the delicacy of the bones beneath the flesh.

Something inside him leapt to meet the sweet nearness of her. He no longer cared what his head had told him — he loved her, that was all he knew, all he cared. That must be enough. Nora had been right, as always . . .

He led her to the sofa, gently stroking her hair back from her face, without speaking, asking no questions. He went to the cupboard and poured her a brandy. Then he went and knelt beside her.

'Look, love, whatever's happened, take your time, and drink this first.' He kissed the end of her nose, tasting the salt of her tears.

At last her breathing became calmer as she sipped the brandy. The strength of his arm brought her comfort.

She said, 'It was after tea. I walked across the park. I wanted to think about things. Somehow, however many people there are there, you can get away from them, it's so peaceful.' She dropped her gaze for a moment, then she looked up at him, 'You see I was a bit upset this morning, you know — I'd never seen you quite like that before. It was almost as if you were giving me the brush-off,' she paused, 'not that I really have any right to expect . . . ' she broke off again . . . 'In the park, I was saying . . . I must have dropped off to sleep, it was getting dark. I got up to go. I had some books to mark up, and I thought you might be back . . . Two men got up at the same time. They'd been sitting on a seat nearby. They were watching me, and they followed me as I walked through the park. I knew they must be because I stopped on purpose near the bridge, where the ducks usually are. And then they stopped too. They pretended to light a cigarette, look at the view, but all the time I could see they were watching me. Directly I started to walk on, they started too. Suddenly I was terrified. I just ran and ran, then I lost my way. I seem to have been running for hours. All the way here. I know it's stupid, childish to panic. But somehow I just couldn't help it.' She looked away for a moment, then said so quietly her voice was hardly above a whisper, 'I've seen them before, both of them. Sometimes together sometimes separately. I'm certain I'm being watched all the time. At first I told myself I was being stupid, I put it down to coincidence, imagination, but I can't now, not any longer, and I'm frightened, Rob . . . '

He sat beside her, drawing her to him. 'There's nothing to be frightened of, little love, not now. They would have come to the door if they intended to . . . ' His arms were tender, gentle. He kissed her eyelids, the end of her nose, the nape of her neck, her mouth. Slowly, she responded, tentatively, as if she were not sure it was true, that this was really happening.

'The sweetness of you,' he whispered. 'God, I wish I could hold this moment forever. I wish you could be with me every evening, letting the day wind down. I wish I could just think you'd be there. Oh Jackie, I love you, I love you.'

In the twilight her skin seemed luminous, her eyes were enormous in her face, their expression, as she looked at him, was one he had never experienced with a woman before, not that he had held many thus in his arms before. It was love he saw there, he recognised it now, love — and innocence. Her lips clung to his with a deep poignancy, her breath caught on a sob as she whispered his name. He held her more tightly as the dusk turned to purple night, and one by one the lights in the mews came on, pools of gold reflected in her eyes.

At last they stirred, he released her gently and got up, putting on one of the lights which had a rose-coloured shade so the light should not shatter the soft cocoon of peace they had wound round themselves, for a little while shutting the outside world away.

'Coffee?'

She stretched like a kitten, 'Mm, please. Lovely.'

The fragrant smell filled the little flat. He brought two big mugs and a tin of biscuits.

'I've had quite a day since I last saw you . . . ' He started to tell her about the state he had found the flat in, the burglary, then about Frank and the bug he had found. He took it out of his pocket and showed it to her, describing how it worked.

'It makes me feel quite sick,' she said softly, 'I didn't believe that such things really went on. It's unbelievable.' She looked at him, the lamplight a halo behind her head, 'Those two men, do you think I was imagining things?'

He shook his head slowly, 'No, I'm sure they are connected with the whole mysterious jigsaw in some way. God knows how. But I don't think they meant you any actual harm. I think they're just watching, waiting. I wish I knew what for.'

She got up and stretched. 'It's long past midnight and I have to be up early in the morning.'

Once more he took her in his arms and kissed her. 'I wish . . . '

She put her finger on his lips, 'Don't say it. Let's just concentrate on present things — there's time, lots of time . . . '

He nodded, 'Yes. You are so much wiser than I am.' With their arms entwined, they went down into the mews. He waited while she unlocked her front door, kissing her again before he returned to his own flat.

He was so tired, it was an effort even to have a bath and, instead of soothing him, it seemed the warm water had the opposite effect, stimulating him into fresh thought, so that he lay, tossing and turning, quite unable to sleep. All the events of the day passed through his mind, in front of his closed eyes, like a film unwinding. And yet they made no sense. The integral part was missing, the 'eye' of the storm, the piece which made all the other bits interlock, eluded him.

At last he got up and made some coffee, taking it through into the sitting room. For some reason his eyes were drawn to the tape recorder. He went over to it, ejecting the tape with Carol's voice. He needed music. Beethoven, Mozart . . . He stood for a moment, undecided, the cassette in his hand. Then, on impulse, he put it back and switched on the machine. It was eerie in the shaded lights of the little room, in the still, quiet of the night, her voice

— Carol's voice — speaking Russian. He played it over and over again, but it yielded nothing.

He wished Jackie were there. She might be able to help. He finished the cold coffee, switched off the lights and went back to bed. At last he fell into a dreamless sleep from which he woke, unrefreshed. He crossed the hall and picked up the morning paper which lay on the mat, glancing through it as he ate his cornflakes. He was about to throw it on the floor, when a single page column caught his eye. He read it without much interest. It was mostly snippets of political jargon and gossip.

Halfway down he stopped. There was a small paragraph which read — 'A rumour is growing that MI6 are involved in a case of national security concerning a foreign personage of some importance. It may be coincidence, but the Russians have been claiming for the past six months that Victor Bolkonski, one of their most eminent scientists, had defected to the West; despite assurances from Britain that he is not in this country . . . '

He read it through twice. An idea was edging its way into the corner of his mind. What had been those initials in Carol's Journals — the part she had typed on loose leaf paper — V.B.? No, V.P. He got up quickly and went over to where her old portable typewriter stood, just as she had left it. He rolled in some paper and typed VP/VP/VP . . . VB/VB/VB . . . the last six letters came out too as VP/VP/VP . . . the key must be chipped so the bottom half of the letter B was missing . . .

He sat down on the sofa, looking at the piece of paper in his hand. Suddenly he got up and raced over to Jackie's flat, keeping his finger on the bell until she came to the door. Before she opened it she said 'Who is it?'

'Rob. Could you come over to the flat, there's something I want you to hear.'

She opened the door and he grabbed her hand. For a moment she held back,

'Rob, I'll be late for work!' She laughed up at him, at his urgency.

'Don't worry. I'll drive you to school, it won't take a moment. Please!'

From the tone of his voice she knew it was urgent, serious. Running before her, up the stairs, he went to the tape recorder and switched it on. As Carol's voice came over, he said 'What is that she's saying?'

Jackie looked at him in amazement. 'Is that it? I told you before, she's asking for some milk. It's just a set phrase in the manual, like 'La plume de ma tante' or 'Buenos noches.'

'Oh!' It was a flat sound. All the tense, pent-up excitement suddenly drained from his face. He sank down into a chair. She went and stood in front of him, taking one of his hands in hers. 'Rob, you didn't think it had any significance, did you?'

'I don't know. No, that's not true. I did I suppose. It's been niggling at me, on the edge of memory. Just a word — listen . . . ' He got up and played it again. She nodded as she listened, then she said, quoting ''Can you help me? I'd like some milk in my coffee'.'

Now suddenly his excitement returned. 'Say it in Russian, say the words . . . '

She repeated them.

'Please, the first phrase again . . . ' He picked out each word as she uttered it, making her repeat it slowly, then faster, over and over again. At last he stopped her in mid-sentence. 'Which word is that, the one you just said?'

'Help — it's the word for help — Please help me . . . '

He leapt to his feet, all the excitement had returned. 'That's it! That's the word, the phrase the man called out — the man at the riding school. I knew it had some significance, it wouldn't leave me . . . ' Now he took the newspaper from the table and pointed to the paragraph.

'Read it!'

She did so, then looked up at him, completely bewildered.

'Don't you see? That Russian,

Bolkonski — he's in Britain. He's the man I saw at the riding school. I'm sure of it.'

'Rob . . . ' she held out her hand. But as if he didn't hear, hardly knew she was there, he went on . . .

'When I saw that paragraph, I knew it had some kind of connection, some significance. Then I remembered the entries in Carol's Journals. It wasn't V.P. like I thought, it was V.B. There was a fault on the old typewriter . . . on the sheets she'd typed. Now I know he was talking in Russian, and I know the word he said . . . it was help . . . help me . . . '

Jackie caught her breath with excitement . . . ' And this is the man Carol was involved with? Is that what you think?'

'I'm certain of it. It all starts to make sense at last. The reason her death was made to look like suicide, all the brick walls I've come up against, the lies, the denials, it's all a massive security cover up. If Carol was working for

MI6 — and I'm sure now that she was — and the Russian found out — there's the motive for murder, and of course MI6 would have to conceal it from everyone, including the relatives of the victim . . . '

'But how on earth had she become involved in the first place?'

'I don't know at the moment. But she worked in Whitehall, she learned Russian — there could be any number of reasons. But the important thing is now I have evidence that she was murdered. And this time I'm going straight to the top. To MI6 . . . '

19

Rob felt the adrenalin coursing along his veins. At last there was some daylight at the end of the tunnel. He was more elated than he had been since he reached England. The fearful part was that the elation was to do with Carol's death — perhaps elation was hardly the word — but it was a feeling of triumph, that he had been fighting some kind of evil, fighting blind against an intangible enemy. Now at last that enemy was going to materialise.

He dropped Jackie off at school. He was going to go through all the notes he had made, everything, every shred of evidence.

As he put his key in the lock, he heard the phone ringing. He picked up the instrument, 'Stanton here.'

'Ah, Mr Stanton. My name is

Jackson. I don't know if you'll remember, we met in Whitehall a short time ago.'

Jackson. He wasn't likely to forget. Carol's boss. A fairly smooth operator he had thought. What on earth could have moved him to phone . . . the voice went on, 'I'd like a word with you if you could spare the time. I was a bit afraid you might be moving on.'

'No, not yet. I should be glad to meet you any time.'

'Well, as they say, there's no time like the present, if you can manage it.'

Rob could manage it. He was certain the man wouldn't have rung him unless he had something pretty important to say . . .

He was ushered into the same office, but this time there were no typists, no secretary — only a man who stood at the window with his back towards the door — and Jackson, who came to meet him, his hand outstretched.

'Do sit down, Mr Stanton.'

As he spoke the man at the window

239

turned. When Rob saw his face he was
so surprised he leapt to his feet. The
last person on earth he had dreamed of
meeting, stood before him.

'French!'

The man bent his head slightly in
acknowledgement. 'Good day to you
Mr Stanton.' He waved towards the
chair Rob had just vacated. 'Do please
sit down. I called you here because I
wanted to have a word with you — at
least Jackson approached you.'

Rob hardly took in what he said, his
eyes were fixed on him as he said,
'There are quite a few words I would
like to say to you too.'

Suddenly he felt relaxed, as if he were
now in charge of the situation. There
was a subtle alteration somehow in the
atmosphere, it was as if he held the
whip hand and they knew it. He
couldn't say why, put his finger on it,
nothing had actually been said, it was a
purely intangible change.

He leaned back and lighted a
cigarette, without seeking permission

from either man. Earlier, he would have done.

As if not to be in any way belittled by his action, French too leant back, lighting a cigarette, watching Rob through half-closed lids. Then he said slowly, with a hint of antipathy in his tone.

'Mr Stanton, I don't think you quite realise what a nuisance you have been making of yourself. You have stumbled into what is one of the tightest security matters my department has ever had to deal with . . . '

'YOUR department?' Rob said sharply.

French paused for a moment, tapping the ash from his cigarette into an ashtray with slow deliberation. 'Of course. I am sorry. I should have explained myself. But I am sure, with your perception, you have guessed I am not simply a riding instructor. My function is as a member of security at MI6; on this occasion, connected with a top priority case.'

'Bolkonski!' The name erupted like a small explosion from Rob's lips.

For a moment the mask-like expression fell from French's face. Then he nodded, 'Yes, but I am not at liberty to discuss the matter. In any case, it does not concern you . . . '

'My sister's death concerns me!'

French ground out his cigarette butt, and placed his fingers together like a lay preacher . . . 'Ah yes; your sister. Now, Mr Stanton, your sister committed suicide. I know it's a hard pill for you to swallow, you have my deepest sympathy, but it is a fact you have to accept, for it is the truth.' His eyes reminded Rob of pale, damp pebbles in a stream. Expressionless, cold, ruthless.

'Then perhaps you can explain exactly why I have been summoned here? Surely not just to tell me you're a top man in MI6? And in any case, what's he got to do with it?' He pointed at Jackson who was looking extremely uncomfortable with the turn of events.

'Mr Jackson is involved in this

particular case in a minor capacity. I felt it better that the 'summons' as you put it, should come from him. After all, you have already met him in his official capacity, and trusted him, as you obviously don't trust me. I suggested you come here, Mr Stanton, to advise you — advise you very strongly, to give up all this foolishness, this quest you have embarked on which can only end in frustration and disappointment. As I said at the beginning of this interview, you have crashed — blundered — albeit unwittingly, on something which is a matter of national security, top priority . . . '

'And may I ask you why you call my 'quest' as you put it, foolish, Mr French? Doesn't my sister's death mean anything to you?'

A small muscle started to twitch at the corner of French's mouth. He was drumming his nails on the leather cover of the desk. Colour flushed his cheekbones.

Rob silently congratulated himself.

The man was losing his cool.

'I have already told you, Mr Stanton, your sister's SUICIDE has nothing to do with us.'

'I disagree, not only disagree, but I have evidence to prove it was nothing of the kind.'

French glanced at Jackson, and smiled. Everything was behind the smile that had been the cause of Rob's frustration. The man gave a faint, derisory shrug of his shoulders and picked up a paper knife, balancing it on one finger. His attitude was louder than words. His contempt for Rob and his enquiry. His knowledge that he was safe within a barricade of red tape, of bureaucracy, of security. 'What is this 'evidence', Mr Stanton?' His voice held chips of ice.

Slowly, methodically, Rob went through every shred of evidence he had, every piece of the jigsaw he had painstakingly dug out — the fact that Carol was learning Russian — the mention repeatedly of 'V.B.' in her

Journals, the fact that she was regularly going to the riding school, the difficulty he had over her car, the fact that Jackie, her neighbour, had said how oddly she was behaving. The way she had changed and how all her friends said the same — Frank and Nora . . .

As he brought forward each point, French refuted them. 'The car was simply a matter of police routine in any case like that . . . as for the initials V.B. — you know how these young girls romanticise these things in the journals they keep — this 'Dear Diary' syndrome . . . as for the riding lessons, that is one of the most usual pastimes I believe, of young girls these days — after the discos. Part of my 'cover' if you like to give it such a dramatic name, is as a riding instructor. Carol met me simply through that.'

Once more he leant back, a smirk of satisfaction on his face. He had neatly, and completely, demolished any case Rob might have, and with plain, inarguable commonsense. Of that he was sure. 'I'm afraid you have taken two and two, and made forty four, Mr Stanton.'

The utter satisfaction in his voice once more got Rob on the raw. But all the man's rhetoric had left him unconvinced. With a small flourish he brought out his trump card.

'Have I? Then perhaps you can tell me how this comes into your calculations.'

He took the bug that Frank had given him from his pocket, and laid it with slow deliberation on the desk.

The two men looked at it. Jackson looked a little taken aback. French merely smiled.

'I'm afraid that is hardly evidence that would stand up in court, or at any enquiry, Mr Stanton. I have never seen it before, and of course there is no proof you yourself have not simply produced it — for sensationalism. In any case, I really fail to see that could have anything at all to do with your sister's death.'

Rob stared him fully in the face, his glance unflinching. 'You really expect me to believe that, don't you?'

Neither of the men spoke. Rob got to his feet. 'I can see it is hopeless to try to get through to you. Whatever I may say, you have already determined not to believe me.' He leant his hands on the desk and thrust his face towards them both, 'Well let me tell you, both of you, I don't care what you think, what you say; neither do I care whose territory I trespass on, I'm going on with my quest, as you so aptly put it, I'm going to get to the ultimate conclusion if it takes the rest of my life, and every penny I possess, however dramatic you may think that sounds. I mean it, because everyone is going to know that my sister did not commit suicide, and why she was murdered, and by whom.'

He swung on his heels and went out of the door, slamming it behind him.

There was silence in the room for a moment. The two men looked at each other.

At last Jackson spoke. 'I wonder how on earth he found the bug.'

French got up, 'Yes, I have to admit that was, to say the least, unexpected, and a bit tricky.'

'Mind you, he wasn't convinced by anything we said before that anyway. You didn't handle that part too well, actually. I'm not sure it might not have been better to tell him something — to leak a little information, as the press has it.'

'No one must know,' the other said sharply. 'If it's found that we have a mole in our midst, at this level . . . '

'True. I agree he shouldn't be told that, but I still think you should have made an effort to be more convincing . . . '

French gave a slow smile. He went over to the window and looked down into the street below where Rob was just getting into the Mini.

'I don't want to convince him. Let him go on. He's doing very well up to now. When — and if — he finds his sister's murderer — then we'll have our mole . . . '

20

As Rob drove back from Whitehall through the midday traffic, his mind went feverishly over every detail of all that had happened in the last halfhour. It had been a shock to find French was so deeply involved with MI6, although he had suspected there was something pretty fishy about him . . . and then, Bolkonski — what a turn up for the book that had been! He felt pleased at the way he had ferreted out that piece of information, put most of the pieces of the jigsaw together — not quite all. But that had thrown even the suave French for a moment. He smiled to himself as he remembered the man's face, and how the mask had slipped.

There had been moments when he could gladly have strangled French with his bare hands; the smug expression, the oily way of speaking, the contempt in his voice and the way he had said, with such arrogance, that Carol had committed suicide. Rob could hear his words now echoing in his mind — 'Your sister committed suicide — I know it's a hard pill for you to swallow . . . ' etc. etc. He had eyes like a fish . . .

Rob knew it was stupid, self-destructive even, to feel so angry, so bitter. But he couldn't help it. He garaged the little car and let himself into the flat. Somehow, after having lived in it for even so short a time, it brought a measure of comfort, peace, a kind of tranquillity. At least the mews was remote from the incessant roar of traffic, here it was only a distant hum.

He put on the inevitable coffee to percolate. As he did so he heard light footsteps along the hallway outside, and guessed it was Jackie.

'Come in and hear all my news . . . '

She glanced at him quickly. He wasn't sure of the expression in her eyes, but she took his hand, and the warmth of the touch of her skin brought comfort.

'Jackson rang.'

'Jackson?' she raised her brows. 'You mean the chap in Whitehall?'

He nodded, and passed her a cup of coffee. For a few seconds he didn't speak, busy with sugar and cream, a tin of biscuits. She shook her head at the latter.

'That's right; and guess who was with him? Well I won't keep you in suspense — French, the chap from the stables.'

Her eyebrows went even higher. 'French? What on earth . . . '

'You may well ask.' His voice was grim. He paused to take a sip of coffee. Then he went on, 'French works at those stables as some kind of cover, that's obvious. And when I mentioned Bolkonski — for a moment I really shook them.' He grinned at the memory, then went on to tell her all that had happened, copying the way French had spoken.

'Jackson didn't have much to say for

himself. It's difficult to assess how deeply he is involved. But there's no doubt they must think I'm an idiot, as thick as two planks.' His voice was savage now, the anger still boiling inside him. 'I KNOW Carol was in some way connected with this Russian chap, and that it was that which led to her death. As sure as God made little apples, and no one and nothing is ever going to convince me of anything different.'

His jaw was set, his mouth in a hard line. Once more she put out her hand, almost as if she were calming and comforting one of the children at school.

'Look, love, I do know how you feel, I can imagine the way they treated you.'

He broke in, as if he hadn't even heard her, 'I'm going to the Press, Radio, TV, the lot. I'm going to blow the whole thing wide open. Some of the recent exposures of moles and so on, are going to pale into insignificance beside the story I'm going to tell them, and help them to find out the rest.

They're the boys for that. They'll leave no stone unturned. They'll know the right avenues to explore in the corridors of power . . . I can just see the headlines now . . . '

Jackie jumped up and stood for a moment, looking down at him.

'Wait — just for a few days, please Rob. I do know how you feel, believe me, you're furious, and rightly so. But don't you see you're going to spoil your own case if you're not careful? Up to now you've been so reasonable, so scrupulously fair in how you have gone about everything, every detail. If you're not careful, you're going to say more than you intend. The press people aren't fools, they've seen this kind of thing before, and they're pretty hard-boiled where this kind of information is concerned. You have to convince them of the truth, put your facts coolly, in cold blood, in an almost detached way if you like; so that you come over as a totally reliable witness, with no hint of bias or hysteria. If they think for one moment there is any possibility, any chance of your being some kind of nut, or crank, you'll be finished before you start. You must be calm and rational.'

For a moment he sat looking up at her. Then he got slowly to his feet and, putting his hands on her shoulders, kissed her gently on the forehead.

'Why is it that so often women are much more rational, more logical, than men? It was almost as if Nora was talking to me then.'

He dropped his hands, and went over to the window. 'Of course you're right. I must wait, prepare my case.'

He swung round. 'Will you help me? After all, you've been in on this since the beginning — before that — because you . . .' his voice broke for a moment, 'you were one of the last people who saw her alive.'

She nodded, 'of course I'll help. I'll do anything I can.'

★　★　★

Over the next few days he prepared his case as if he were going into court to defend himself. It was going to be detailed, coherent, an exact description of every single thing that had occurred since the moment he landed in England — a perfect presentation of the evidence that Carol was murdered.

Each evening Jackie came to the flat straight from school. He would have a meal prepared. He found he quite enjoyed buying the ingredients, and trying his hand out at some of the recipes he'd found in a book on the shelf. Sometimes, as he measured out the ingredients, he could almost hear Carol's voice telling him about the different dishes, some of which she had picked up on holidays abroad. And, all the while, his mind was going over the weeks, the days, the hours he had spent on his investigations.

He made out endless lists, subdivided them, taking all the information from the first lists he had made, making new headings, talking to Jackie about everything she could remember about Carol in those last few days and weeks, particularly in the light of the knowledge they now had. At her suggestion he made two piles of notes, one with the actual concrete evidence, for which he could supply times, dates, names and facts; and the other of the suppositions, the conclusions he had drawn.

At the end of the week, he felt sure that he had done a really good job on his 'case'. He grinned at Jackie, they were both quite worn out with talking, writing, discussing, but one evening he said. 'I think this really is convincing. It is well presented, though I do say it. I have read it right through, trying to take a completely objective view. I honestly can't find any holes in it.'

He had cooked them steak au poivre, with fresh peas and new potatoes, a bottle of hock from the fridge; fresh strawberries and cream completed the meal. Jackie smiled at him over the rim of her coffee cup. 'I thought this must be some kind of celebration. Quite honestly, another week of this luscious food, and I should have got too fat to get into any of my clothes.'

For a moment he covered her hand with his, looking serious again.

'I couldn't have managed it without you, without your encouragement. Tomorrow we go to the Press, the whole media. There can't be much doubt now, with maximum publicity, they will have to re-open the case, and at last we shall have the truth out in the open.'

He got up and started to clear the table. Together they went into the little kitchen and washed the dishes. Both of them were now used to putting everything away in its proper place.

'I think we deserve a little relaxation,' he said, 'and a glass of brandy.' He poured two glasses, then, having passed one to Jackie, went over and switched on the television. 'There's a documentary on South America, the part where I

257

was, I want to watch. Do you mind?'

Before she could answer, the telephone rang.

Rob lifted the receiver. As the voice came over the wire, he put his hand to cover the mouthpiece, and whispered to her, 'It's French . . . ' He beckoned her to come. She got up and went to stand by him so she could hear the conversation. French was saying . . . 'It's really something that had occurred to me, after our conversation in Whitehall the other day, Stanton. I felt there was a matter I would like to discuss with you in private.'

'We have nothing to say to each other,' Rob said shortly, 'I thought I made that perfectly clear on the last occasion when we met . . . '

'Now look here, I know I was a bit short with you, even a touch unreasonable, after all it was a very serious matter you were talking about, a serious accusation shall we say; or at any rate, you inferred as much. And you must admit, Mr Stanton . . . ' Oh ho, Rob thought, I'm given a handle to my name now am I? French was going on, 'You must admit, you didn't give either Jackson or myself much chance to . . . well to reply to those accusations, for which, I may say, we were totally unprepared.' His voice now was conciliatory, almost apologetic, for his former attitude and behaviour — probably because he was lying, Rob thought, but he also got the impression that something must have happened, or some conversation must have taken place which had made him more than willing now to listen to Rob's story. It seemed curious, but in view of the fact of the case he had now prepared, he felt more than ready to utterly convince the man of the truth, as he knew it to be.

'OK,' he said coolly, and without showing too much enthusiasm. 'Do you want me to come to the office again, or are you coming here?'

There was a slight pause, then French said, 'Neither, I think. There's a place we use sometimes, it's not difficult to find. I can quite easily explain if you have a pencil and paper handy.' Jackie went to the table and brought the notebook and pencil they had been using.

'It's a turning off the Commerical Road — not far from Stepney Station, a right-hand turn . . . ' Jackie wrote down the details as Rob repeated them. Then he said, 'When? Now? Why not, it can't be too soon for me. I'll see you in about half an hour then.' He replaced the receiver and turned to Jackie.

'Do you know I honestly believe I've got through to him after all!'

He picked her up and swung her round, like a small child, making her chuckle with delight then, setting her down, he said, 'Come on then, give me those directions, I wasn't taking a lot of notice. Hope you've got them down OK.'

'Of course. But there's no need for me to give them to you. I'm an excellent navigator, as you already know, and I'm coming with you.'

He turned round in the act of putting on his jacket which lay on a chair.

'I don't think that's a very good idea, quite honestly. He did say 'privately', and whatever happens, I don't want to blow this. I feel the whole thing is highly — well — tenuous, that's the only expression I can use for it.'

She stood stubbornly in front of him, shaking her head. 'No, Rob. As you said just now, we've been through all this together, all the way through. I don't want to be left out now. It wouldn't be fair. Please?'

She looked up at him like a small girl, her eyes pleading, but there was a tenseness about her mouth.

He grinned and, putting his hand under her chin, lifted her face towards him. She could sense the excitement that coursed in his blood, ran along his nerves, communicating itself to her.

'OK Partner . . . bring your map and compass . . . '

21

It seemed to be further than they had thought. The evening traffic was thick. Several times they were stuck in a jam. Rob drummed on the steering wheel with his fingers, glancing at his watch.

'I suppose we *are* going the right way.'

Jackie nodded, intent on the map and the directions.

'Yes, we've done all the turns we should have done, we turn right here and it's a few yards down the road.'

He pulled the car up in front of a building which had once been some kind of warehouse, odd pieces of corrugated iron were nailed here and there over gaps. There were gaping holes in the roof, the windows were dirty and many had no glass, pieces of board had been inserted in a haphazard manner. Jackie gave a little shiver.

'This can't be right. It's part of the old docks, been out of use for ages.'

'It certainly is odd but, as you said, we've followed the directions he gave us down to the last letter. This must be it. At least it's private like he said.'

'I'm not surprised,' Jackie said, 'look at that old boat, all that's left are its ribs . . . ' she pointed in the sleazy water which lapped the edge of the road. All kinds of flotsam and jetsam floated on the surface, old tins, pieces of rag, bits of timber, an old shoe and something which looked horribly like a dead cat.

'Perhaps there are some offices inside, you know, the kind of place one sees in all the best spy films, hidden away here so no one would have any idea they were there at all.' He turned to her now, 'I'm going to put my foot down though. You're not coming in with me. I don't know why — perhaps it's the state of utter decay over everything, but I'd rather you stayed in the car. Honest.'

She gazed round as he spoke. It had

started to rain, big thunder drops, and navy blue clouds were massing down river. Already there was the sound of distant rumblings heralding the coming storm. 'It's a bit spooky, old docks always are. One keeps thinking of the time they were busy, teeming with people, ships coming from all those faraway places; men shouting. Now they're just dead, deserted. OK, I'll sit here and listen to the radio. Don't be long — and good luck. I'll keep my fingers crossed.'

He bent and kissed her lightly on the lips. Then he got out of the car and went towards the side door — the one French had described, although he had never imagined when he specified a side door that it was a warehouse. These people certainly had odd ideas. When one read about them in books, one thought the whole thing was being over dramatised, made melodramatic for effect. Maybe it wasn't all so far from the truth after all.

The door obviously hadn't been used

for some time. The hinges gave a loud squeak of protest as he pushed it. Once inside it was dark as night, then, as his eyes got used to the gloom, he saw it must still be used as some kind of storehouse for he could see vague shapes in the twilight, mostly covered with plastic sheeting. He took a step forwards into the murk, wishing he had brought a torch. There was one in the car. Should he go back for it? Then he thought there might be some argument with Jackie if she thought the place was so odd that he needed a flashlight.

'French!' He shouted the name. It was given back from the high vaulted roof with its broken panes, a mocking echo which reverberated round and round as though he had called half a dozen times.

He waited a few moments. Eventually the echoes died, there was complete silence except for the distant hum of traffic, and the lap of water somewhere beneath him. A ship gave a distant, mournful hoot on its siren, adding to the eerie atmosphere. He shivered and began to wish he hadn't come. Once more he shouted the man's name . . .

Suddenly he was blinded by a light full on his face, dazzling, making him shut his eyes. 'What the hell? Is that you, French? What are you playing at for God's sake!'

He opened his eyes. A man stood in front of him. It was as if he had literally materialised out of the gloom.

'I'm glad you came so promptly, Stanton.' The 'Mr' had been dropped again.

Rob saw French standing there. He waved his hand around, 'This is a bit melodramatic, isn't it? Been reading *Smiley's People* have you?'

But French was not now to be drawn. He grinned and replied, 'I did tell you there was a need for secrecy, and no one would dream of looking for us here.'

Suddenly Rob thought that rather an odd, even menacing, remark. Why should anyone want to look for them?

And who? . . . But French was going on, 'As you know, I've suggested we met so you and I could have a little talk about your sister's death, or, should I say, her murder!' He walked over to a couple of broken chairs in one corner of the warehouse. 'Would you rather sit?'

For a moment Rob was so surprised by French's words, his admission at last that Carol had been murdered, that he was thrown off balance. He stood rooted to the spot. French turned, slightly impatient now, 'Well?'

Rob shook his head, 'No thanks, let's just get on with it shall we?'

French shrugged his shoulders, 'As you wish.' He put the torch down on one of the chairs. Its light cast bloated, nebulous shadows in the darkness, among the shapes of the crates and boxes. He lighted a cigarette without offering Rob one. 'As a matter of fact, your theory was perfectly correct, if it brings you any satisfaction, which I doubt. However, Bolkonski had been helped to defect, on the understanding of course, that he would talk about his work, tell us the information we needed. The usual arrangement. But once he was, as he thought, safe in this country, he clammed up, not to put too fine a point on it. When these cases occur, which is not unusual, we have to use . . . ah . . . other methods.'

He stopped and studied the end of his cigarette with exaggerated concentration. Rob got out his packet and lighted his own cigarette. He rested a foot on one of the chairs, hand in his pocket where the notes he and Jackie had made were in an envelope. He had brought them in case there should be any argument. He wanted to have his own evidence absolutely crystal clear. He was almost disappointed they were not going to be needed.

French continued, 'We have many methods — some legal, some perhaps sailing a little close to the wind. But many years ago any form of physical torture was abandoned and we do not go in for killing agents, contrary to what some of the popular fiction writers would have us believe. Oh no, we have other, much more civilised, methods. In this particular instance it was decided to soften him up, and this was where you sister came into the picture.'

Rob had thrown his cigarette away now. Its tip glowed on the broken cement floor like a small scarlet flower.

'As you know, she had a good job in Whitehall. She was intelligent, utterly trustworthy — and innocent, in every sense of the word.'

Rob could feel the anger inside him start to rise like a flame. Soon it would overwhelm him if he wasn't careful. Somehow he had to keep a check on himself until he had heard the full story, until he had his proof. But it wasn't easy, as the man went on talking in his hateful, detached, cold manner.

'Above all, she was about the age of Bolkonski's own daughter, whom he adored, and who was in Russia with her mother. He wanted desperately to get them over here. Also he enjoyed horseriding as did your sister. We arranged for her to study Russian, enough to get by. She was quick to learn. And so by degrees, as they rode together, and talked, he came to trust her and began to talk about his work.'

Rob broke in. 'And did Carol know what she was doing?'

French studied the end of his cigarette once more, decided it had burned down far enough, and lit another from the stub. Rob was seething with impatience. 'I asked you a question. Did she know what she was doing?'

'That is something I cannot answer, Stanton. As I said — as you know — she was an intelligent girl. Anyway, the plan worked. Of course the Department was pleased.' He paused again, 'That is — all except one, unknown, member. There had been suspicions for some time that there was a mole among our number who was working secretly for the Russians, and of course when Carol was found dead, then suspicion became certainty. The local police were on to it like long dogs. They soon found she had been murdered, and that meant MI6 had to move in immediately, in a desperate attempt to cover things up. At all costs there must be no scandal. Our tame medic, Dr Hackworth, whom you met, testified that she had committed suicide. The Home Office agreed to cover up, and everything went according to plan. Permission, and instructions of course, had come from the very top. You will, I am sure, realise the implications, the complications that would have arisen had the truth ever emerged. And then of course, out of the blue, you had to turn up!' French's voice now had a hint of bitterness.

Slowly Rob said, 'You could hardly have expected me to let matters rest. In fact, obviously you didn't or you wouldn't have had me under surveillance.'

French inclined his head. 'We hoped you would believe she had committed suicide. Then the police told us you had been asking questions. It was then we had you tailed. We couldn't afford to have this affair brought out into the open.'

'And was it MI6 who burgled my flat?' Rob asked.

'Yes. Jenny Lapford, the girl you met in the 'Blue Duck', told us about the Journals, you had spoken to her of them. That was a piece of bad luck for you, Stanton . . . ' Rob stifled an exclamation. To think he had suspected Jackie! 'So now you know the full story . . . '

'Then why the hell didn't you tell me all this at Whitehall instead of this cloak and dagger bit?'

'My dear fellow, because I can trust no one. Jackson — anyone, could be the mole. If I had admitted you were right, it is more than likely your own life would then have been put in danger. You see you really do know too much, Mr Stanton . . . '

Rob shook his head. 'There is still

one piece missing. The most important piece of all. This mole, my sister's murderer. I still don't know who he is. And I won't rest until he is found, until the whole thing is brought out into the open and Carol's name cleared.'

'I thought that would be your reaction. You run true to form.' French made a sound, half-chuckle, half-triumphant. For some reason the sound made Rob's blood ran cold. It sounded sinister, eerie, in this dim place. Suddenly he saw the flash of metal in French's hand, and the barrel of a gun was pointing at him.

'That is exactly why, Mr Stanton, I cannot of course allow you to leave here. Sooner or later you WILL discover the identity of the mole. That would be most awkward . . . for me!'

Rob had no time to think even. He knew he was in deadly danger, and self-preservation made him automatically swerve towards the chair where the flashlight stood. He knocked it over, and it smashed on the floor as he heard the sound of a muffled shot and felt the wind as a bullet whizzed past his head.

He turned, desperate, blind, stumbling, tripping, banging his shins against crates and tin boxes in his headlong flight. French knew the place, he didn't. He had every advantage — and a gun. He heard his footsteps right behind him. Suddenly he came up against a blank wall. Somewhere there must be a door. He ran along the wall, his hand outstretched. Once more he heard the sound of the gun and a pain like searing fire hit his shoulder. He sank to the ground. There had hardly been any sound from the gun, no echo in the deserted warehouse. A silencer of course . . . he waited now for the third shot . . . could it be French had himself got lost in the near darkness? If only somehow he could let Jackie know where he was so she could go up for help . . . He started to crawl along the floor on his hands and knees, he made no sound . . . and then the idea came to him.

Painfully he dragged himself to his feet, then he shouted, 'Over here, French!' Once more the gun was fired from some little distance. Rob immediately ducked to the ground again. Just as he had planned, the bullet hit the corrugated iron of the wall and the sound reverberated round and round the warehouse, unlike the original shots . . .

'Please . . . dear God . . . let her hear . . . '

22

The storm still rumbled in the distance, but the rain had stopped. There was the tense, stifling, heavy feeling there often was before a storm actually breaks. The static made Jackie yawn as she sat in the car. She glanced at her watch. Rob had been gone ages. She had thought it would only take a few minutes.

She switched off the radio. Punk music wasn't her scene.

Suddenly a shot rang out. She jumped out of the car, glancing round desperately for help. She realised immediately how absurd to think there would be anyone in a place like this. Rob was in great danger. She had suspected something of the kind from the beginning, that was why she had wanted to go with him. Now she had to find someone . . . She got back into the car and drove back the way they had come. A phonebox . . . she snatched open the door . . . it had been vandalised, the instrument on the floor, the cord ripped out . . . suddenly she realised how stupid she was being. By the time she found anyone who would listen to her story, or rung for the police, it would be too late. Rob would be badly hurt — perhaps even dead.

She swung the car round again and drove to the big main doors of the warehouse which they had passed on the way in, before they reached the side door French had described. An idea formed in her mind. Suddenly she had become quite clear-headed. She had to help Rob. Only she could do it. There was no one else. If there had been, they would have appeared by now, at the sound of the gunshot. He was some-where inside that rotting building, in deadly danger. Rob, whom she loved, who meant everything to her, more than life itself.

She had been through all this before, losing someone who had been the centre of her world, so that for a time she would have welcomed death, even invited it. That was not going to happen again, not if there was anything in her power to stop it. She would rather lose her own life than be without him . . .

* * *

Painfully, inch by inch, Rob had managed to crawl behind one of the crates, every nerve screaming as he waited for the inevitable to happen — French to find him. This time it would be at close quarters, and he couldn't miss.

Glancing round the side of the packing case, he could see a darker mass in the gloom. French creeping towards him.

Suddenly, with a noise like a bomb exploding, the rotting doors of the warehouse burst open as a car crashed through. French swung round at the sound and Rob, forgetting his pain, leapt to his feet.

278

Jackie was stumbling out of the car. By some miracle she had managed to open the door of the battered vehicle.

'Look out!' he shouted then, as French turned towards him, he leapt on the man and, with his good hand, smashed him on the wrist. With a howl of pain, the gun fell from his hand. Then French threw Rob to the ground and raced for the door. Rob picked up the gun and raised it, praying there was another bullet. He was about to pull the trigger when a voice shouted.

'Hold it! We've got him!'

Hardly able to believe his ears, stupefied now with pain and loss of blood, he dropped the gun as Jackie came up to him. Dizzy, he leant on her.

'Rob, my darling, are you all right? Where did he shoot you?' Before he could answer, a light went on and they turned round . . .

'Jackson!' They both exclaimed at the same moment. Jackson nodded, and turned his torch on the two uniformed officers who were putting handcuffs on

279

French. 'OK Sergeant, take him away.'

Rob looked at Jackson. Faintness came over him in waves, but he managed to say, 'I suppose I should ask how the hell you got here? But quite honestly, nothing more can surprise me tonight, although I must say, some explanation would be nice.' He tried to grin.

'Well,' Jackson said slowly, 'unknown to our friend here,' he jerked his thumb in the direction in which French had been taken away by the police, 'I had my men tailing you, Mr Stanton, for I knew perfectly well you were entirely unconvinced that day in Whitehall. In fact, French didn't intend you should be convinced. He was playing a clever game, double double cross, and he nearly got away with it. But in my job you neither trust, nor believe, in anyone . . . '

'I seem to have heard all that before,' Rob said faintly.

'Yes, well, that's why I didn't tell even him you were still being followed. So of course, when you went into the warehouse, we approached from the other side, with the help of the river police. There's an outside iron staircase which goes up to the loft above here. We heard everything, and were about to intervene when Miss Fremington . . . ' he turned and nodded at Jackie 'so adroitly entered the warehouse and made our job much easier . . . ' They went towards the door where French, now securely handcuffed, was being bundled into a police car.

'What will happen to him?' Rob asked slowly. 'As you are so keen to have no scandal, I suppose none of this can be made public. But surely he won't just get off scot free. The man's a bloody murderer!'

Jackson shrugged his shoulders. 'I shouldn't worry your head over him, Mr Stanton. He'll go where he deserves. Maybe he'll even wish he'd been hanged . . . '

Rob looked at him enquiringly as the man broke off, then went on, 'the

Russians can have him. I hope he enjoys his stay in Moscow, because he'll be there for a hell of a long time, come snow and high water, as you might say.'

'But he still won't have been punished for Carol's murder!' There was a note of desperation in Rob's voice, almost a sob as he said the words.

'Not publicly, no. That would bring the full story out into the open.'

Rob looked at him hard, defiance in his face as he said, 'I could still go to the media. I have the full story now.'

Jackson looked straight back at him. 'We shall deny everything,' he said, simply. For a full moment the two men stared at each other as through they were sizing themselves up in a boxing ring. Then, suddenly, as if on an impulse, Rob held out his uninjured hand, and Jackson took it in both his, a smile on his lips as Rob slowly shook his head. The other man released his hand, and then, taking him gently by the elbow, said, 'Come along young man, you've lost a lot of blood. We must get you to our surgeon without any more delay.' He turned to Jackie. 'And you'd better come along too, young lady. I rather think that car's a write-off, but it was a nice piece of driving.'

Thankfully, she nodded, her knees beginning to feel a bit weak now it was all over. She followed Rob into the back seat of the car. He was feeling very faint and shaky and sank back thankfully as they drove off.

The surgeon sent him to hospital for a check-up after he had dressed the wound. Fortunately the bullet had only grazed it, but the flesh wound had bled a lot and they gave him a blood transfusion and kept him in overnight to make sure there was no infection.

Next day Jackie drove him up to see Nora. He had already been on the phone to her, and she had insisted they come to stay, at least until his arm had healed.

As soon as they arrived, she made them eat an enormous lunch, and then the three of them had driven to the little country churchyard where Carol was buried. Nora and Jackie stood a little to one side while Rob knelt and put the huge bunch of flowers Nora had picked from the garden, on the grave. Red roses, pinks and carnations, sweet williams . . . 'All the flowers she loved.'

Then Rob stood up and put his good arm round Nora's waist, as she said, 'I'm glad we know the truth, love. For some reason it makes her death easier to bear.'

He nodded, 'It was the one thing I couldn't — wouldn't — accept, that she had committed suicide. I knew it just wasn't true, not in her character. Now I'm content, and somehow I think she is too. Those who loved her know the truth, and really that is all that matters.'

Now he turned and took Jackie's hand, and the three of them walked slowly through the little graveyard, with its moss-covered headstones, the waving summer grass, thick with moon daisies and poppies, the sweet smell of the summer afternoon hung over all.

Rob said softly, 'Jackie and I are going to be married, Nora, once I can find a job in this country.'

Nora looked up at him, squeezing his arm. 'I had hoped for that. You've made me happy, bless you. I never did want you going back to that heathen place either.'

Rob smiled. 'It wasn't all that heathen, but now I know where I want to be, England, especially now.' He turned and gently kissed Jackie on the lips, holding her close for a moment. They walked on to the lychgate. Rob opened the little iron gate for Nora to pass through.

'Remember how, as kids, we used to say this was a wishing gate, and someone must open it for you so you didn't touch it as you went through? I don't think it was a proper one really, but we liked to think so. In some ways, anyway, a wish has come true. I couldn't bring her back, but at least I could do this for her and, in doing so,

Ifound another kind of happiness . . . '

He followed them both through the gate, pausing for a moment to look back at the grave with its bright flowers. Then he closed the gate and said softly. 'Come on then, let's go home . . . '

THE END

Other titles in the
Linford Romance Library:

YESTERDAY'S LOVE

Stella Ross

Jessica's return from Africa to claim her inheritance of 'Simon's Cottage', and take up medicine in her home town, is the signal for her past to catch up with her. She had thought the short affair she'd had with her cousin Kirk twelve years ago a long-forgotten incident. But Kirk's unexpected return to England, on a last-hope mission to save his dying son, sparks off nostalgia. It leads Jessica to rethink her life and where it is leading.

THE DOCTOR WAS A DOLL

Claire Vernon

Jackie runs a riding-school and, living happily with her father, feels no desire to get married. When Dr. Simon Hanson comes to the town, Jackie's friends try to matchmake, but he, like Jackie, wishes to remain single and they become good friends. When Jackie's father decides to remarry, she feels she is left all alone, not knowing the happiness that is waiting around the corner.

TO BE WITH YOU

Audrey Weigh

Heather, the proud owner of a small bus line, loves the countryside in her corner of Tasmania. Her life begins to change when two new men move into the area. Colin's charm overcomes her first resistance, while Grant also proves a warmer person than expected. But Colin is jealous when Grant gains special attention. The final test comes with the prospect of living in Hobart. Could Heather bear to leave her home and her business to be with the man she loves?